Fata Morgana

Svetislav Basara

Fata Morgana

A COMPENDIUM OF SHORT FICTION

TRANSLATED BY
RANDALL A. MAJOR

 DALKEY ARCHIVE PRESS

LIBRARY OF CONGRESS CATALOGING-IN-PUBLICATION DATA

Basara, Svetislav, 1953-
 [Short stories. Selections. English]
 Fata Morgana / by Svetislav Basara ; translated by Randall A. Major. -- First
edition.
    pages cm
 ISBN 978-1-56478-195-6 (pbk. : alk. paper)
 I. Major, Randall A., translator. II. Title.
 PG1419.12.A79A6 2015
 891.8'236--dc23
                2015017524

This translation has been published with the financial support of the Republic
of Serbia Ministry of Culture and Information

Partially funded by grants from the National Endowment for the Arts, a federal
agency, and the Illinois Arts Council, a state agency

www.dalkeyarchive.com
Victoria, TX / London / Dublin

Dalkey Archive Press publications are, in part, made possible through the
support of the University of Houston-Victoria and its program in creative
writing, pulbishing, and translation.

Cover: design and typography by Arnold Kotra
Composition by Jeffrey Higgins
Art by Katherine O'Shea

Typography: Mikhail Iliatov

Contents

Through the Looking-glass Cracked

1

"What kind of beginning is this?" asks the typesetter at the printer's, as he reads "What kind of beginning is this?" He waves his hand in resignation and continues to set the text. Thus, the novel begins at a moment when it was already finished long ago. Yet, the discussion in the novel began much earlier: it began one night when I realized I did not come from an ape.

That night, my world fell apart.

Until then I had always had considerable self-confidence and self-respect. Evolution, history, science, the Party and the Association of Young Communists supported and encouraged me. As such, I was something of an improvement over the apes: I knew how to read and write, to add and subtract, and I had learned my fractions as well. I knew how to shout out slogans like "Hurray for a Better Tomorrow" and "Down with the Inhuman Regime," and for that period in our country's history, this was all quite sufficient. If the Holy Spirit had not personally told me in a dream that I had been created from nothing, I would have enrolled in the College of Mining and Geology and made a career for myself somewhere deep under the earth. But Providence had other plans for me. I was supposed to write a novel. Why was I the one chosen? I will always ask myself that, but I will never find the answer. The ways of the Lord are mysterious.

Thus, in the place of a pithecanthropus, nothingness became my only ancestor overnight. I felt it on my very skin. I was the commonest sort of "Speaking Subject" and, as such, I existed only due to Käte Hamburger, *The Logic of Literature*, and to a certain man named Neuse. I was introduced by him "into the definition of tense by means of the concept *speaking subject*, and thereby into the system of tenses or into the system of reality (which are the same).* More precisely, I existed only in my own novel. In the outside world nothing was possible for me. It was 1949. The time of construction and renewal. There was nothing out there for me.

However, a serious problem arose: my language refused to speak. Having grown accustomed to decrees and directives, it dared not say a word about the things I wanted to write about. For example, if I were to start the novel with the sentence "My family started to disintegrate," the words would immediately qualify themselves by adding "but it was an outmoded, bourgeois family anyway." I did not know any other languages, but I am convinced that the situation was quite similar among them as well. All languages are inherited from corpses; generation upon generation of corpses continue to spread their lies through the words which are still in circulation. How can one write, then? In spite of it all, the little skeletons of letters began to organize themselves into necropolises made up of lines, like the skeletons of the dead, testifying that X Y and Z were trying to live but were not doing so well. This analogy helped me a great deal in the first days of my nothingness. As a matter of fact, no one manages to live, even though that is everyone's basic goal. Using the argument "What about those who kill themselves?" will not work: they kill themselves precisely because they are not able to live. All of us die, leaving behind either a large or a small pack of lies. Those packs of lies gather together after a while, and from them emerges the history of human society and culture.

Encouraged by such meditations, I slowly achieved self-consciousness. "All right," I figured. "I don't exist. Nothing can be done about that. Whining and complaining won't help. Being envious won't help. That is all just a waste of time. In the final analysis, no one exists. The heated battle ends in defeat. Would it not be better to surrender in dignity, to admit defeat at the outset? All events in my life have one common goal—my death. Whether good or bad, they are just another tile in the mosaic of my biography, another bit of litter on the heap of rubbish that remains after life."

* Käte Hamburger, *Die Logik der Dichtung*, Stuttgart: Ernst Klett Verlag, 1957; pg. 29.

These revelations had a considerable calming effect on me. While you exist, you are blinded by differences. You would rather decide to be a psychiatrist than a madman, a malefactor than a victim. But all of those paths are the same: they lead straight to death. One day you die and you see that you never even existed, that there were no traditions, that nothing was worth all the effort invested. And then it is too late to change your mind. You become a loyal subject of history — a corpse.

2

In the beginning, I had long conversations with my father. My decision to not exist he did not like in the least. To be honest, my father was not a bad man, perhaps he was a bit overambitious, but that did not help him: after certain horrible tribulations he turned into a rubber doll, even though he held on blindly to his faith in medicine. My father's death held a certain kind of satisfaction for me. Maybe it is not polite to say that, but the roots of evil lie deep in a man even though he does not exist. My father wanted to know who Heyse was. He thought Heyse was the one to blame for my fixation. I could not help him. Neuse had always worked from the shadows. Through quotes and footnotes. He never slept because he was the enemy.

"Come on, Ananias," my father began, "What's the point of all this? You know very well that it is not 1949. You can check it in the papers."

"Newspapers don't mean a thing. You can print whatever you like."

"You've read somewhere that the best novels arise from neuroses and now you are simulating neurosis so that you can write a novel. It will do you no good. You have no talent."

This was absolutely true. But I did not want to admit that. The basic rule is "never admit anything." My own father taught me that, as his father taught him, and his father before him, all the way back to Adam.

"What is it that you really want?" he asked.

"I want to dis-indoctrinate myself."

"What is that supposed to mean?"

"Look, we are all indoctrinated. We are indoctrinated to believe that we are people, that we came from apes, that we exist, that we know something, that we are good, that we will be happy. You're indoctrinated to believe that you're my father, I'm indoctrinated that I'm your son. We are both indoctrinated that the Earth revolves around the Sun, that the capital of Romania is Bucharest, that the boiling point of water is 100° Celsius. You're indoctrinated that you want only the best for me, that you should talk with me, that you are worried about me . . ."

My father took his head in both hands. With this gesture, he was trying to arouse pity in me. It did not work. On one hand, I felt sorry for him: he had been indoctrinated into believing that taking one's head in one's hands will arouse pity. On the other hand, I was completely indifferent because I did not exist. There were no longer any emotions there. Anyway, deep down in his soul, like any other father, he never really tried to understand me. In the end, how can you trust someone who sleeps with your mother? That should always be kept in mind. Being a father — it's just an excuse for a fellow to sleep with your mother. Our fathers have hung a halo on that doctrine, and the emperors to whom they bow have granted them a Magna Carta that allows them to sin.

"Can you explain it to me?" my father asked.

He meant dis-indoctrination.

"Perhaps I could, if you have the time to hear me out."

My father blurted out a total lie:

"Of course I have time for my own child."

"Look, Dad," I said, "we are all empty inside. I don't deny that we all exist objectively. But this table and that chair exist just as much. Inside, deep within us, there is nothing. Ontologically, there is no difference between you and Mickey Mouse."

"Is that any way to talk to your father?"

"You said you wanted to talk."

"Yes, but not like this. I didn't think you would compare me to Donald Duck or Mickey Mouse."

My father's pride had been hurt. He was not upset by ontology. Not that. For him it was unfair that Mickey and Donald appeared in the newspaper every day. His own name would appear at rare intervals, during big celebrations, always near the bottom of the page. I wanted to tell him that, but I remembered the commandment "Honor thy father and mother . . ." and so I said something else.

"I'm afraid you don't understand it. You are taking the game too seriously. You are playing. To play means to imitate, to imitate means to ape. An inversion has come about: we did not come from apes, we have become apes . . ."

"Stop!" cried my father. "Speak for yourself. I came from an ape. Understand? I CAME FROM AN APE!"

He said it twice. With extra emphasis on FROM AN APE. Just in case the walls had ears. He wanted the walls to hear that he was completely convinced that he had descended from apes, so that the walls would carry the message to his superiors. Having stated his "credo," my father looked at the walls to see if they were satisfied. The walls winked back at him in comradeship.

"All right," I said. "You're free to believe what you choose."

"Just tell me where you read all this nonsense."

"I didn't read it. I wrote it."

"You wrote it? You're incapable of that. That Heyse fellow has filled your head with a lot of nonsense."

My father sat down on the floor and pressed his hands to his ears. This whole scene was put on to arouse pity in me. But his gestures had no effect. Even though we were not talking anymore, he sat there for the next forty minutes . . . in complete silence . . . in order to arouse boredom in the reader.

When he left, he stopped at the door and said, "No one will want to read such a boring novel."

3

From the very beginning, my mother tried a different set of tactics. That is quite understandable. Women are indoctrinated to be gentle, compassionate and sensitive. The doctrine makers had an interest in it being so. It is just an act, all that gentleness, I am sure, but their acting is more sincere, more convincing. Although it is just as destructive as arrogance, compassion is at least tolerable. Consequently, my mother tried to convince me that I existed through my favorite foods. I ate them — to eat is not the same thing as to exist — but not with the appetite I had once had. After you realize that you do not exist, you lose a good part of your appetite because you are constantly aware that when you eat you are fattening up your own corpse. But my mother was satisfied. If you are eating, you exist; that is what she thought. Unlike my father, she did not need verbal declarations about belonging to the phenomenological world. She never believed that I actually did not exist. She thought it was just a passing fad. My grandmother and aunt concurred. They thought that I was going through puberty and that I had an *idée fixe*; which was basically true, since every human idea is an *idée fixe*. Once you make that connection, then it becomes quite clear to you that nothing exists.

My father was at odds with this whole non-existence business. He sat in his wicker chair in the corner, flipping through his daily *Workers' Struggle*, making sure that I could always see the front page, which showed the date. He even made an attempt at some rather subtle psychological terrorism. Now and then, for example, not addressing me directly, he would ask out loud: "What's the date today?" as if he were not sure. If I was the only one in the room, I would say "July 23, 1949," and he would become upset. If someone else was present, I would keep quiet, and they would give the date. I never paid much attention to this because I knew they were trying to indoctrinate me. I faithfully clung to my July 23, 1949. On that day I had not yet been born. For that very reason I clung to that time of my redemption. For others, time was passing; for me it was not. No longer would I play that silly game with clocks, deadlines and seasons. I knew time was passing, I just did not care. When you stand by a river, you know it is flowing past, but you feel no obligation to turn and follow its course to the sea. Time is different, because of indoctrination. The rules of decency demand that you move with time, shoulder to shoulder, until you die, and then time goes on. No one has ever reached the end of time. Yet, my father acted as if he would actually get there and receive his laurels. Perhaps he was behaving that way under directive, but the fact remains that he behaved like that, and there are no excuses. He did not let a single date slide by. Every few minutes he would ask what time it was. As if he would fall behind by 24 hours if he skipped over that one date, that one moment, in his race with time. When he went to bed, he always knew what day had just passed and what day was yet to come. He prided himself on it. Many years later, when my father had disappeared on "the byways of destiny" (as he liked to say), when all of our conflicts remained in the past, on the rubbish heap, I got carried away with the idea of putting up a magnificent bust of my father in the central town square to spite the mayor. The bust would show my father in top form, looking—with a serious expression on his manly face and with that self-assured countenance so characteristic of people who believe that they come from apes, of those who never miss a chance to vote and are never late to work—looking, as I said, with a definite socialist-realistic expression at the clock on the church belfry, full of delight because he could watch the passing of time which made him happy most of his life, and which convinced him that he existed. However, I gave up on the project. Partly because my father was converted near the end, partly because I really did not want to fool with the sculptors, and partly because I completely forgot about it with the passing of time. Mostly because of the latter. But, *in illo tempore*, my father continued to rudely shove the headlines of *The Workers' Struggle* under my nose, to show me that time was indeed passing. I never really doubted the passing of time. I do not know why he needed to do that. They played dirty tricks like buying me a watch for my birthday, even though I had moved back into the time before I was born. It was a beautiful Russian watch, the brand was START. I will never forget it. My father only bought Russian things. I wore the watch for my mother's sake. I could tolerate it. That was a small thing in comparison to what I was supposed to be tolerating.

The novel was moving on. The first chapters, wrenched away from the time of my father, were running on like sand through the hourglass. There was no future before them, nor was the past gaping behind them. Neuse was pulling the strings, I was doing the writing. All in all, I was satisfied. Except for one detail. In the novel, a sentence appeared which was not written by *me*. The sentence said "Marina has blue eyes."

4

Right at the beginning of the fourth chapter, my father burst in on me.

"I want us to talk," he said.

I wanted something else to happen in this chapter. I did not plan on a conversation with my father. But I agreed. After all, he was my father. I could see that he felt uncomfortable. He was missing something. It was time and space. "Fictional time," writes Käte Hamburger, "present, past and future characters in a novel, are transformed into an event only if they are dealt with in narrative-stylistic means. The same is true of space, which only appears in the novel when it is mentioned." No kind of space had been mentioned; July 23, 1949 did not fit in with his understanding of dates; nothing had been transformed into an event, and that was not the way my father liked things to be. He noticed that I had seen right through him. So, he purposefully got up and wanted something. But it seemed to him that he had not stood up purposefully enough, so he sat down again and then stood up even more purposefully. However, he then forgot what he had wanted; so he sat down again.

"You see," he said, "I have not become as obtuse as you imagine. I read something about the Cabala. In one place there it says 'Man, do not pretend that you are an apparition because you will turn into an apparition.' What you are doing looks dangerously like you are transforming yourself into an apparition."

Obviously, he did not like the idea of being the father of an apparition. I did not think badly of him for that. I did not even doubt that he had read something about the Cabala. However, I was sure that he had done so under orders from above.

"Dad, you misunderstood me. The prejudiced belief that you

exist is founded on a false projection of reality. You are mixing your objectivity with your subjectivity. I already told you that you exist objectively, but subjectively there is absolutely no difference between you and Donald Duck."

At this point, Donald Duck mysteriously appeared in the room. Winking, he pointed over his shoulder at me with his thumb and said to my father, "That's what he said. I heard him."

"You'd better shut up, duck!" screamed my father.

"Listen," I said, "don't shout at Donald. It's really not his fault. Just like you, he is one of the characters in my novel."

My father simply could not get that into his head, the fact that he was being equated with Donald. This only proves how false his tirades about equality were. He grew crimson with anger. He was on the verge of tears because of his hurt pride. He wanted to say something else, but then he remembered that the walls might report to his superiors that he was talking to Donald Duck, so he changed the subject.

"Can you explain the bit about the wrong projection again?"

"The thing is, you are never just one. There are always at least two of you. The first is on the surface, the second in the depths. The first is your own creation, constrained by the limits which doctrine allows. It is something artificial. That is why you are never enough for yourself. You are always missing something and you must seek affirmation. You are looking for something in the world, you are looking for yourself in others, at conferences, in the wrong direction. Whenever you seek for it in the right place — inside yourself — you immediately flee in panic, because there's nothing there. The indoctrinated YOU is different from the real YOU."

My father was squirming in his chair. I said *in his chair* intentionally so that he could have a place to sit. That made things easier for him. Every father needs a little space. But this time, he tried no theatrics. He did not even try to force his opinion on me. This proved that man is not an existing being, that he is impermanent, characterless, that he changes according to the situation and to the whims of everyday politics.

"The things you've said contradict reason," my father said.

Ratio had spoken out in my father. And not only *ratio*: all the materialists, the Cartesians, Enlighteners, and Encyclopedists— all of them spoke out through my father from the depths of history.

"I'm glad to hear that," I said. "I want to contradict reason. Reason rules the world. There's not even a shred of irony in that. And what kind of world is it? Tell me."

"To be honest, things in the world are not the best, but capitalism is to be blamed for that. When the world revolution one day brings final victory, the Earth will be like heaven. Everyone will work as much as they can and get as much as they need."

There's the rub, I thought to myself. My father is luring me onto thin ice. He's waiting for me to say something against the world revolution so that he can report me. In that case, they will censor my novel without a second thought.

"It's not that I doubt in the world revolution," I said hypocritically. "But that is a long process, and this is a metaphysical matter. You and the others like you have constructed a world where you feel safe, where you are protected by the secret police, the courts, the insurance companies and all the other nonsense. You've constructed a world where—like drowning men grasping for straws—you grasp for the orthopedic devices of continuity and newspaper headlines. This is pure self-deception."

"Go on, go on," he urged me, as if he were interested.

At that moment I saw through his dirty little trick. He wanted me to get carried away, to blurt out something unsuitable or, if nothing else, to drag out the monologue, thereby tiring the reader. That was probably why he came to talk to me. He was forcing this conversation into the novel to replace other interesting events. His calculation was actually not so naïve: if the reader, having had his fill of metaphysics, closed the book, then I would lose and he would win. On his side, he had the whole phenomenological world, the enormous propaganda machine. On my side, I had just a few readers. I am forced to make a promise: there will be boxing and blood in the pages to come. I had to do something. But I also had my trump card: by presenting my reflections in the form of a conversation with my father, presenting him in such a dim light and thereby generating sympathy for myself, I achieved a greater effect than if I had put this all in the form of an essay, which was my initial intention.

So, I went on with my metaphysics in order to make the best of the moment:

"The pyramids, don't forget, are slowly turning into dust. The time in which they were built is eating into their rebellion against eternity."

"You're starting to overdo it," Donald Duck whispered to me.

For some inexplicable reason my father jumped from his chair to the top of the cabinet. Up there, behind the jars of homemade candied quince, he was laughing and crying at the same time. Joyfully, for once again there was space. If I had only wanted to put the real date instead of July 23, 1949, I am convinced he would have hugged me and taken me to the zoo so many years too late.

5

In spite of my ontological convictions, I started playing soccer for the Radnički Soccer Club. The coach, management, and fans had nothing against my beliefs. They were only interested in whether I made goals or not, not whether I existed or not. And I was making goals. It was quite miraculous. The only one who was really disturbed by my career in sports was my father. He wanted me to find a respectable occupation; to be a police inspector, an army officer or, if nothing else, a machine engineer. While jogging and building up my stamina at team practices, I came to an amazing conclusion. Using psychoanalytic methods I realized that my father was a *sturm und drang* type fellow, and that it was not possible that he was uninterested in sports. Something else was at work: everything I did, if it did not fit in with his wishes, brought him into a state of horror and made him mortal. Because, unconsciously no doubt, my father intended to make himself out of me. Not in the sense that I was to be a copy of him — it was not that. He wanted me to become him completely, to take on all of his traits, to accept his beliefs, his virtues and his faults, so that he could die in peace, certain that he would continue to live on in the form of me. So, just to spite him, I played soccer with all my heart. He believed that soccer is a corrupt game. And, admittedly, he was right. However, I was not playing in order to be corrupt — I had been corrupted enough already — I played so that I could find some sort of identity (for instance, the number eight on my jersey), and to learn something more about history. Soccer is a typically historical game; like history, it makes no sense. Kicking a ball across a goal line makes no sense whatsoever. The only way for a man to be sad or happy in today's world is indeed to grieve when his opponent scores a goal on him, and to rejoice when he himself makes a goal, alternately grieving and rejoicing, together with a vast crowd of nameless fans, their common bond being a great relief in itself. That is how far things have come with grieving and mourning. However, that is in the domain of sociology and it does not interest me at all. The similarity between soccer and history is different in nature: to win at all costs, to win regardless of the victims, regardless of fair play. "Fair play" is a charming error of the Baron de Coubertin, which the reprobates have taken advantage of and capitalized on. I have played soccer and, I swear, there is no fair play whatsoever. It is all just one fraud right after another. When you trick the opposing team's halfback, the crowd is on its feet cheering you on, but you do so by committing one of the deadly sins: your opponent thinks you are going to the left and you go to the right, and Satan exults in the clouds above the stadium. You rush down the sideline and your only thought is: "deceive them, deceive them, make a goal." Once, after I had already hung up my spikes and I was only occasionally sparring with my friend Boba, I thought up a more humane version of soccer in which you could get to your opponent's goal only through better knowledge of certain sophisticated subjects: music, poetry, geometry and so on. This was, however, just a sports fantasy. Personally, I would not be able to play even in the lower leagues. It would just never work. The dynamic of the game is what attracts fans. Not justice and truth. Is it just to look at one corner of the net and then kick the ball into the other? To shame the goalkeeper who is, after all, just a man under his uniform? It is not, of course it is not, but the fans and the media extol the goal-maker, thus shoving him straight into hell, which is full of professional soccer players, along with all the others. Fortunately, I grew bored with the whole thing rather quickly. When you know that you are nothing, it is not that easy just to grab onto something. I quit playing soccer, and avoided the eternal flames by a hair.

This all happened around the time my aunt made her first trip to England to visit her brother, about whom there was some doubt as to his existence. Her supposed brother was just an excuse to get a visa. Nonetheless, my aunt soon wrote us a letter from there. Included with the letter, there was also a picture. In it, she was sitting in my uncle's yard, at a table covered with all kinds of chocolate, coffee, ham, bananas, olives—all those things which were never seen on our table. "Lucky her," said my mother, looking at the picture. "It's all just propaganda," my father said. "You know, it's like that wall portrait at the Adriatic Photo Shop. We had our picture taken there once. You stand there under a palm tree and they snap your photo! It's the same thing in England. You go to the studio, sit at a table full of delicacies, they take your picture and then you send it to your relatives. In reality, outside the shop, people work eighteen hours a day, and small children are forced to pull the carriages of the capitalists." And yet, that very evening my father secretly got out of bed and wrote my aunt a letter. He wanted her to bring him some powder blue pinstriped material for a new suit.

6

The day when I told my family at lunch that I had decided to be born again, they decided to lock me up in an insane asylum. But since everything was done according to a plan at that time, I cannot discount the possibility that they put me in the madhouse under a directive. It is possible that in some law somewhere it said "If he wants to be born again, lock him up in an insane asylum." They mustered up the courage to do it with heavy hearts. Not because I was not insane, nor because they felt bad about it, but because something else was at stake — their reputation. A black cloud looms over the families of the mentally insane; people look on mental illness with reproach, and you really have to overdo it to make your family stick you in the nuthouse. Everyone is crazy, there is no doubt about that. But families hide the fact to the utmost limits of their patience. I did feel sorry for my mom, I am not insensitive. The fact that she had given birth to me meant a lot to her, because she could put a highly respected title by her name — mother. She was even a good mother, I do not want to be misunderstood, I have no objections to her. But the birth she gave me was incomplete and sloppily done. That is not her fault. No one can give birth to anyone *completely*; people are imperfect, women especially, although the ideologists claim otherwise. If you really want to live you have to give birth to yourself, to pass through that tortuous process again, to agonize, in order to have the right to say "I am alive" and not have the heavens burst out in thundering laughter. I am sure that they would have turned a deaf ear to the directive as well, and would have continued hiding my insanity, if only the walls had not heard my proclamation. But they did. They could hear even quieter statements than that. After I said "I want to be born again . . ." the walls made a horrible face, full of nausea. My father was stuck between a rock and a hard place. My mom started crying.

"I did everything I could for you," she said through her tears. "I don't know what was wrong with the way I gave birth to you. You were a beautiful baby. You weighed ten pounds. You didn't have water on the brain or a harelip."

"Mom, don't take it so seriously. You did your part the best you knew how. I'm not complaining about you. But I just can't stop there. Perhaps it is arrogant, but I am a perfectionist."

"You're a madman!" interjected my father, hiding his face behind *The Workers' Struggle*.

Perhaps he was still grasping at a straw of hope that I would notice the real date in the headline and stop pretending. He was convinced that I was pretending. Those who are really pretending cannot believe differently. I know this from my own experience.

I ignored my father.

"Look, mom, this body is too crude. It is only raw material. It must be redone. It's not good to be satisfied with that which exists. A person can always do better."

"A person!" cried my father maliciously. "I thought that you didn't exist. That you were nothing."

"One has to start from nothing," I said.

"You will start at the insane asylum. If you don't want to go for a psychiatric examination, I will report you and they will come and get you."

Of course, the walls reported our conversation, word for word, to higher places, and the police, firemen, civil defense workers and public services were all prepared to help my father, just as he would have helped them. The solidarity of fathers is miraculous. So, just to keep from making a mess of things, I said that I would go for the examination on my own. And I did just that.

7

There is no insanity like that which exists when a psychiatrist and crazy person get together. Like a husband and a wife make a marriage. It takes two to create real nonsense. It just does not work otherwise.

I sat across from the psychiatrist. There was insanity between us, it brought us together. But I was crazy Ananias, and the psychiatrist was the psychiatrist. Those were the roles assigned. The doctor was supposed to convince me of that, and the problem would be solved to everyone's satisfaction.

The doctor had a goatee á la Freud. But that is a superfluous detail. Freud had already completely indoctrinated him, completely permeated him, turned him into himself and was comfortably living in the form of the doctor, under the doctor's name. I did not think badly of the doctor for it. I left that to the ideologists. They create doctrines, turn people into themselves and live in them like parasites, because they are incapable of being born again and living as individuals.

The psychiatrist observed me perfidiously. The moment you step into the office, you are crazy until proven otherwise, or unless you have an influential uncle. I had no intention of proving anything. He took my silence to be a capitulation, and admitted me into the psychiatric ward. To our mutual satisfaction. He liked me even more because I confessed everything right off. Even so, he kept me there in his office for a while. He had to stick to form. He could not just send me off to the psychiatric ward. Because of the walls, of course.

"Ananias, I will be honest with you. I think I know the root of your problem. Things are like this: your father is a powerful person. He has, shall I say, *swallowed you up*. You can find no way to step out of his shadow and establish your own *I*. So, you have decided you don't exist. The calculation is simple and logical, but it is sick. You think to yourself 'If I don't exist, if I don't have my own *I*, then my father has no influence on me.' In other words, since you can't fit into reality, you've decided to leave it."

The doctor was not that stupid after all.

"Everything you say is completely correct," I said.

Deep from within the doctor's soul, the late Freud was exulting in the doctor's face. Idiotically, one must admit, but that is the way ideologists exult.

"All of that is, I say, true, but my father is actually a weakling. Perhaps he looks manly at the rallies. I cannot deny it. He takes the directives seriously, and if the directive says 'Be manly,' he will be manly. However, he gets up at night and secretly eats candied quince in the pantry. My grandma will tell you it's true. When he gets drunk and my mom and grandma scold him, he cries like a baby."

"You can't look at things that way," said the doctor.

And that was it. The doctor had fulfilled his duties. We both did our jobs to the best of our ability. That was what he was paid for. I was given a bed, food, medicine and psychiatric care. The best thing about the whole nightmare is that you are compensated. You suffer a bit, but at least your belly is full.

A little later they bathed me, cut my hair and killed me; they operated on me, covered me in powder and put me in bed.

That evening, Käte Hamburger visited me. Since I was officially crazy, there were no legal reasons to hide it. No one is upset by the hallucinations of the mentally insane. We could talk about literature in peace.

"Mr. X was on his way," I said secretively.

"You see, from the novel I would not learn," said Käte, "that he *was* on his way, but that he *is* on his way."

"Why?"

"In the novel, the grammatical tense of the preterit loses the function of giving information about reported facts in the past."

"That's defeating."

"Quite rightly it is said: a phenomenon is a consequence without a reason, an effect without a cause. It is hard for one to find cause and effect, because they are so simple that they are hidden from sight."

Here the conversation ended. The sleeping pills began to take effect and I fell asleep. But I continued to write the novel in my sleep. A handful of barbiturates was not something which could knock me off my stride. I had dreamt somewhat similar dreams before, but this one was quite clear. I could repeat every word I wrote verbatim. The dream was so clear that I thought I was not sleeping at all, so I went to see Kowalsky. He was a friend of mine, and I will tell you more about him when I wake up. I asked him how he was, how his children were, what he was doing. He answered that he was fine, the kids were fine, he was not doing anything in particular. We sat in his room and drank coffee, chatting about banal things. Then I set off for home by the same road I use when I set off for reality. Along the way, I even met some acquaintances. They nodded their greetings to me, quite unaware that it was just a dream. To be honest, I was not aware of it either. It was only when I got home and sat down to lunch that I noticed my grandfather sitting with me. This was nothing unusual, but it was unusual for me. When I finished my soup, I remembered that my grandfather had been dead for ten years. I realized I was dreaming and I could not eat any more. I went into my room, and in the dark, groped at things and bumped into them, looking for my bed which was not in its usual place but in some other place altogether, and it was even possible that there were no beds in that room at all, so I decided, tortured by the length of the sentence, to go to sleep leaning against the wall, hoping that the wall did not differentiate *up, down, left,* and *right,* but the wall did differentiate them quite well; there were no walls anyway, that was not what it was all about, so I thought: maybe there is not a bed in this room, maybe I entered the wrong room, so I went out into the hallway where there were two rows of identical doors on each side, and I was no longer in any single room, and that decreased the chances that I would finally go

to sleep and made the position I would sleep in even more difficult—it is hard to go to sleep if you do not know where you
are—but I did not quit hoping that a context would finally be
found, and there was still a chance that I would find myself even
though it was late and a little awkward in the dark to find, groping around and bumping into things, the room which I was actually in—I rejected outright the possibility that I was not in any
room—and then the notion crossed my mind that I had fallen
asleep long ago and that I was only dreaming that I was search-
ing for the room where I was, located in this endless hallway, so
I thought: great, I will stand *right here* and wait till I wake up,
but I could not define that *right here* in a space where there were
countless, identical doors, and it took me quite a while to understand the hopelessness of my situation, to understand that the
hallway had neither a beginning nor an end, that I was only an
undefined character in part of a sentence whose content I could
not even begin to fathom, a sentence wrenched from the context
of a fateful story about which I knew nothing. But the confusion
did not last too long. Not nearly as long as the sentence. A context was quickly found. "Ananias," I said, "you are only dreaming." Instantly it was my room. Dejected, I sat down by the window and waited to wake up, to finally open my eyes and look at
the street which was wet from the rain.

8

When I woke up, I looked out the window. The street was wet from the rain. I tried to remember what I had dreamed. Usually I simply cannot do it, but that morning I did. All of the dreams that I can recall have one thing in common: they are normal, uninteresting, and there is nothing fantastic about them. The most ordinary kind of mimesis. They would pass Soviet censorship with no difficulty. I do not know if that is good or bad. I suspect it is bad. Dreams were once the connection with higher worlds. Now that connection has been broken. Indoctrination has crept into our dreams. Everything has merged into banality. Our paths cross in our dreams, we call out our greetings, we chat, we nod our heads like clowns, we exchange pleasantries, hopelessly imprisoned by the solitary confinement of our own indoctrinated *I*'s.

I went to visit Kowalsky again.

"Imagine," I said, "what I dreamed last night. Like, we were sitting at your place drinking coffee. Afterwards, I went home and saw my granddad at lunch. Before that I saw several friends of mine on the way and they said 'Hi' to me. Absolutely no one noticed that it was a dream."

"What time could it have been when you left my place?" asked Kowalsky.

"I guess it was around two-thirty."

"What's so strange about that? People were coming home from work. They were tired, preoccupied by their worries. That's why they didn't notice that you were dreaming them, that it was nighttime and that they were sound asleep."

"It could have easily happened that I didn't notice either. Thanks to a nightmare from the past, I woke up and somehow managed to wait for myself to really wake up. If that hadn't happened, I would have ended up at lunch, I would have gone for a walk and then gone home to write my novel. In the evening, I would have gone to sleep in my dream, and then awakened in the same dream and everything would have gone on, only on the other side, like when you turn a glove inside out."

Kowalsky laughed.

"But at least you would finish your novel."

"Forget it. I will never finish the novel."

"Why?" Kowalsky asked.

"I don't believe in it. Not anymore. You can read *War and Peace* in a few days, and the action takes place over a period of many years. Because time has been so unbearably prolonged, people resort to means of beautifying and accelerating it. But all of that is *pompa diaboli*, all the novels, history books, and films. That is why I don't hide anything; I have no plot, there is no mystery. Everything is known: you will ride off on your bicycle, far away; Marina will never come. My father will turn into a rubber doll. Boba will be killed. It is pure insanity, if you ask me, to accelerate that process. On one hand, everyone wants to live as long as possible. On the other hand, everyone wants to make the little bit of time they have left go as quickly as possible. We are absurd creatures."

"Precisely," Kowalsky said. "Listen to what happened to me. Once I was waiting for a bus at a remote bus stop. I was not alone. There was someone standing next to me, someone I will not name, for they may read your novel one day. What I mean is that the circumstances are not important: the point is that I had to go and she had to stay. It could not be otherwise, I had to go because I have a highly developed sense of responsibility. You would have stayed. I know. But that is also not important. You see the point: I was chewing my nails, cursing the carelessness which caused the bus to be late; I was wishing that something, which I had never wanted to end, would end as quickly as possible."

"And then?"

"Then the bus came. Listen carefully: I got on the bus, want-ing to get to my final destination as quickly as possible, even though I didn't really want to go anywhere. If there was anything I wanted, it was to remain forever at the spot from which I had departed. But I was chewing my nails, nervous because the bus was moving so slowly. It's always that way: I want something to end so that something worse can start and then I grieve for the things of the past. That's what memories are made of."

"Yes," I said. "That's what memories are made of. But there is a way to get rid of them. And I don't think it is so complicat-ed. You have to slow down. Memories force us into new events. The world is ruled by ghosts and specters. I'm quite sure—you just have to stop. Let's say you are attracted to a girl. Your first re-action is to wish that you were close to her. Wrong. It's better to think paradoxically; getting closer is just the flip side of growing apart. You know what I mean. I approach it differently: I retreat so that I might draw closer."

And indeed, perhaps to prove it, or for some other reason, I began to back up.

"You're thinking of Marina!" shouted Kowalsky.

"Marina who . . . ?"

At that moment, I woke up in the madhouse. Käte Hamburg-er had gone. My lunatic colleagues were waking up. Then an or-derly burst into the room. He looked morosely in the direction of my bed and said:

"Ananias, to the doctor's office."

9

I had been assigned to a different doctor. The great maestro only did the important part of the work. Afterward he let the rest be done by aides who, understandably, were paid less for it. But, however many of them there were, Freud was living comfortably inside all of them, leaving them with the sweet illusion that they themselves were living. The doctor assigned to me was a handsome fellow, over six feet tall, well-read, but he had a cunt. He suffered secretly because of that.

"Ananias, you are an intelligent boy," he started by flattering me.

I could have guessed that part. Flattery is the first phase of indoctrination. The most pleasant. But it never lasts long.

"I say, you're an intelligent boy. You are completely aware that you are simulating your neurosis. So, you are not sick, but this can grow into sickness. So, I've decided to quit pumping pills into you. You have to resolve the conflict yourself."

I already said that the doctor was well-read and humane within the boundaries of doctrine. Everything he said was grammatically correct. But I had no intention of resolving the conflict. Conflicts can never be resolved. At best, a compromise can be reached. I wanted to destroy reason, and even if the price for it was to spend my life in the madhouse, I was willing to pay it. I told him so openly. There was no reason to lie.

"Can you explain that to me a little more thoroughly? Believe me when I say I'm interested."

"What good will reason do me, me for whom it is reasonable to die? Not to mention the other details."

"But to die is neither reasonable nor unreasonable. It is natural." The doctor was defending death. He was, unknowingly, an advocate for the dead rationalists. An ideologist in general.

"Your reason tells you that?" I inquired.

"Yes."

"To live forever, is that natural?"

"No, that is not natural. Not a single case of eternal life has ever been recorded," the dead ideologists echoed from inside the doctor.

I changed the subject.

"Tell me, doctor, if someone were to present the following case, what would your diagnosis be? A man eats nothing for forty days, he scorns worldly goods, he knows that he will be killed and he does nothing to avoid death, he always chooses the harder path, he preaches that evil should not be resisted . . . Is such a man sick or not?"

"He is sick, most certainly."

"He is Jesus."

"Who?"

"Jesus Christ."

The doctor was in a tough spot.

"It was thought that Jesus was God and . . . It is a myth."

"Quite in the spirit of the doctrine: it is thought that God does not exist. But if He does show up, He will be locked up in an insane asylum."

The doctor laughed. He did nothing to show that he was losing his patience. He did not spend all those years in college for nothing. That is where he learned to control himself.

"We shall meet again," he said.

10

Human reason is really excessive. And imposing. It destroys every living word, it breaks every entity down into atoms, and then it makes atomic bombs out of those atoms, only in the end to raise its voice — the voice of reason — against those very atomic bombs. You do not have to be very crazy to see through that. It is a dirty game. Babylonian confusion. Psychiatrists speak psychiatrically, engineers speak engineeringly, and maniacs speak maniacally. You can no longer communicate with anyone.

I was sorry my father did not come to visit me. Not because I missed him. Far from it. I needed him as a conversationalist, as a partner in dialogue, so that I could express my message more effectively. However, the sly old fox felt that it was not opportune to appear at this time and — as a tactical maneuver — he did not come to visit me even once, although I am sure that he would have come because his duties required that he do so. Now, that was just the way it was; I had to say everything in the form of a monologue. I clambered up on my bed, cleared my throat a couple of times to attract the attention of those present, and began to speak:

"My Fellow Lunatics: We have sunk so deep into the absurd that the only way out seems to be in returning to the most absurd of all absurdities which was, in the name of human logic, rejected by rationalism; it is the return to a belief in the immortality of the soul, in the hope for the worldwide resurrection of the dead, and in the eschatological transformation of the world. Do we have anything to lose at all except for our reputations in the eyes of our psychiatrists? Can we be more definitively insane, can we become more incontrovertibly *nothing*, if we begin to believe in the opposite? Ever since the Renaissance, belief in one's own transience and mortality has increasingly become a question of honor, and now it is impossible to find a respectable man who does not frown derisively at the very mention of immortality. In the name of truth, nothing exists which would indicate immortality. Yet, on the other hand, there is also nothing to argue for the finality of death. Both of the hypotheses are equally unproven. To choose one or the other is not, therefore, a matter of healthy reason, logic, or enlightenment, but rather a matter of *faith*. In other words, it is a choice.

"Therefore, my fellow lunatics, the road to salvation must begin with the children's chant 'I don't want to play anymore.' In support of that statement, there must be an absolute resolve to leave the game, an intention to be crazy. It is worthwhile for us to despise this world's system of values. Negative individuality most of all. All of us exist much less, we are much more meaningless than we could ever dream of, even in our wildest dreams. The game is ever the same: vanity. Only the players change from time to time. The secular system of values is based on empty abstractions. A pound of gold is worth neither more nor less than a pound of crap. The real values are hidden behind the Potemkin villages of the phenomenal world. In order to reach them, we must deny ourselves."

The other patients responded to my speech with frenetic applause.

Hearing the uproar, the hospital aides came running to room number 6 to see what was happening. When they reached the door, they could only see me putting a period at the end of the tenth chapter. They were left powerless in the face of the logic of literature.

11

I was released from the insane asylum because the tenth chapter was finished. It simply ended. My father didn't think it was fair. He didn't believe I was well yet. But there was nothing he could do. He talked with his influential acquaintances, he threatened the director of the Department of Psychiatry. All in vain. The logic of literature was merciless. In spite of his own best intentions to meet my father's needs, the director did not want to get involved in literary matters. He knew that, in such a case, he would be a madman and not a psychiatrist, and he did not want to give up his nice salary, his reputation and all the other nonsense just for the sake of my parents' desires. As for me, I quit insisting so much that I did not exist. I realized that one-sidedness is a barbaric trait. In the insane asylum they had brainwashed me a little, I must admit; the doctors are not so naïve after all. I was even ready to make a compromise with the empire, to make a deal where the relationship between something and nothing was 50:50. But I did not want to admit that to my father. That would have been a big mistake. He was insatiable.

The sly old fox felt the ground slipping from beneath his feet. Straightaway he came to see me in my room, full of good will, understanding, and all the other junk from the storehouse of history.

"So," he said, "you're back home. I hope you aren't going to go on with your nonsense. I am interested in one thing though: how did you manage to get out of the nuthouse? That fellow Heyse must have helped you."

He always said "Heyse" for "Neuse," and "Kate" for "Käte."

"No, father. The chapter ended and that was it."

I was telling him the truth. Things are finished up easily

enough. The protocol is secondary. First they condemn a man to death, then they type up the verdict; first they shoot him, then the doctor pronounces him dead. All of a sudden you get out of the madhouse, your release papers and other things are reconstructed afterwards.

"The bit about indoctrination . . ." my father began to beat around the bush. "Could you tell me some more about it? I want you to explain it to me in detail. Perhaps I have been wrong."

A more naïve man would have fallen for such a provocation. Not me. My father was using my own weapons against me. He realized that his behavior and statements so far had aroused antipathy in the readers. Now he wanted to appear to be a man of broad vision, like a martyr. His reaction came too late. Indoctrination was no longer the focus of my interests. My phase of unhappy consciousness was behind me. After getting out of the nuthouse, I mostly thought about Marina.

"No, father. I think it's pointless. It's all just empty words. Wouldn't it be better if we just forgot the whole thing and went fishing tomorrow?"

He saw that I intended to bring another chapter to a close and it really angered him. He wanted to talk some more. It must have flattered him to appear on the pages of a novel. Even if it was an absurd novel.

"Don't you think," he asked, "that this chapter will be too short?"

"No. Long, short, those are categories in Aristotelian logic. It doesn't interest me in the least."

"It will be too short anyway. You'll see!"

"*Dum enim imaginatio,*" I said, "*rationi rerum visibilium formas repraesentat, et ipsam ex earumdem rerum similitudine ad invisibilium investigationem informat, quodammodo illuc eam conducit quo per se ire nescivit.*"

12

Boba was a boxer. We were roommates. I had no idea how we had gotten together. What were the goals of destiny? Maybe it did not have any goals. Maybe destiny does not exist at all. Boba believed in destiny. And it took its revenge on him. But he was not a bad guy. Not at all. He was training, I was writing, and basically we got along. Sometimes I sparred with him. I rang like a gong every time one of his twelve-ounce gloves, stretched over his gigantic hand, hit me. We loved that sound. Whenever it sounded—gooonnnng—he would stop punching me and hop about the room with his hands over his head. He was practicing the art of winning. His goal was to become a professional and to fight against Cassius Clay in the world famous Madison Square Garden. So he had also devoted himself to studying English. In the afternoon you could hear him repeating *"My father is a schoolteacher; I learn English; my mother is a bookkeeper."* He was learning fast, he was not stupid. But, like everyone else, he had been indoctrinated to succeed in life. That was why he was boxing. At that time you could achieve recognition as a policeman or as a boxer or soccer player. Outstanding workers were already being noticed less. That was due to the infiltration of western influences, black music, and fashion.

I did not spend all my time with Boba. Sometimes I would go home; once I spent a couple of weeks with a coed who was studying classical literature. But our idyllic scene was brought to an end by her father. He burst in one morning with a pistol, red-faced and shouting, and he threw me out. I did not blame him. It was his duty to defend his daughter's honor, just as my father's duty was to keep me from returning to nothingness. They had made their calculations: they needed someone to live on through after death. Fear magnifies things. Fathers of daughters are in an even worse situation than the fathers of sons. It was mid-December, I had nowhere to go, so I went back to Boba. "Ha, you're back again," he said and made me breathe in his face to see if I had been drinking. Like all boxers, Boba was a patriot, an athlete, and he totally abstained from alcohol. I only drank in the company of women, and at that time it was usually vermouth. He put the gloves on my hands and hit me two or three times. Then he asked me to hit him. I hit him in the nose as hard as I could. He wiped away the blood and said: "You're not so bad." That was the end of the whole affair.

Boba had read the first five chapters of my novel. I did not know what he thought of it. I do not think he liked it. I have already mentioned that he was patriarchal in his views. He was a war orphan. He had no mother or father and that is why he deified them. And yet, he did not reproach me at all. As opposed to most people, he could see the difference between reality and literature. Once he asked me, "What does that mean '*Dum enim imaginatio rationi rerum visibilium formas representat, et ipsam ex earumdem rerum similitudine ad invisibilium investigationem informat, quodammodo illuc eam conducit quo per se ire nescivit*'?" He had a really good memory. Until all the right-crosses and uppercuts rattled his brain. He had a great talent for philology. If philologists had been in fashion at that time, we would have had another Nietzsche. "That is Richard of San Victor," I said. "The quote in translation says: '*Because while the imagination presents, to our mind, the forms of visible things in the present and prepares it, on the basis of similarities of those things with invisible things, to probe the invisible, the imagination, in a way, is leading the mind along a path which it did not know how to follow by itself.*'" Boba looked at me in wonder. I neglected to tell him that I had placed that very fragment at the end of the eleventh chapter, as a response to my father, as well as to impress the coed whose father had so cruelly separated me from her because I was intruding on his territory. For the sake of demystification, it should be said that 90% of every novel is like that: it all serves to impress or indoctrinate. It is unavoidable. Even being fully aware of all the forms of indoctrination is no help. It is just one more in a series of doctrines, like in my case. I asked him once, "Boba, what do you think of my novel?" He thought about it for a while and then he said, "I think it's boring." That was what I had been afraid of. To break up the monotony, I suggested that we spar a bit. While I was still ringing from Boba's punches, I thought, "Is it any better now? Is the action more exciting?" The masses love boxing. I could count on the sports-oriented readers. But all of that, to be quite honest, was unimportant: to write a description of a boxing match is just as inappropriate as reciting Whitman in the ring at Madison Square Garden. When I think about it, I was living with Boba just to make the action more interesting. To live with a boxer means to live in the constant fear that you will be knocked out, and it is out of fear — says Käte Hamburger — that the most beautiful lines of prose are written.

In January (Boba claimed that it was January) we had two girls over at our place. Boba drank a quart of vermouth. From somewhere in the room, he pulled out the latest issue of *Sports and the World* and showed our guests an article written about him. Above a photograph of his swollen face, there was a big headline:

"BOBA KNOCKS OUT ADEMI IN THE SECOND ROUND"

The girls were delighted. They had been cretinized even more than Boba and I had. Probably because of the original sin. "He's writing a novel," Boba said, singing my praises. In order to keep the demon of glory from going to my head, I immediately admitted that I had recently been released from an insane asylum. But it was too late. The girls had already started to hang on every gesture and on every word I said, they wanted to leave the best possible impression on the readers. They knew that it could all be used against them, that everything would be published sooner or later. Of course, intimacy was now out of the question. Boba had definitively messed things up. A boxer! Nothing could be saved anymore, not in this chapter at least. Knowing this, I decided to just get drunk. Over vermouth and soda-water, I reflected on my hypocrisy. A novel is always better than its author, everyone knows that, but I had shouldered an enormous burden: on one hand, I spat upon the world of everyday events, and on the other hand, I behaved like everyone else: cretinized, I had indoctrinated myself into believing that I did not exist. But I behaved as if I did exist. I did not reproach myself. Nobody behaves in accordance with their doctrines.

"I ran him into the ropes . . ." Boba was saying, "and then I hit him with a right cross and then a punch in the plexus and BANG he hit the mat like he'd been mown down." The girls were delighted. Boba drank a little more vermouth and then went to throw up. I told them it would be better if they left because Boba was not nice when he got drunk. They said, "Okay. Well, good-bye!" And they left. "Where are they?" asked Boba when he came out of the bathroom. I said that they had left. "Whores!" grumbled Boba and went to bed with his shoes still on. In the morning he grumbled something else about whores and went to his training session. *Someone* had already decided to kill him. Nothing could be done about it, chronologically, it was still too early. From that time forward, everything fit into a puzzle which, when assembled, would show a picture of Boba, massacred, lying on a pile of issues of *Sports and the World.* Boba did not suspect anything. He came back from his training session, asked me how the novel was going, and got to work on his English. I heard him reading, "*To day is Monday. To morrow will be Tuesday. To day I learn English. To morrow I will go to cinema.*" To make the absurdity even greater, he had mastered the future tense, even though he did not have much of a future. That is the difference between my novel and the usual novels. In these pages, everything is known. Within the limits of gnoseology, of course. There is no mystification, no hope that something will happen, some miracle. Boba will soon be killed, the investigation will reveal nothing, the perpetrator will remain at large. As if nothing at all was going to happen, Boba fried seven eggs, opened up a can of liverwurst, cut himself some bread, poured a glass of milk, and began eating, dreaming of the day he would finally do battle with Cassius Clay in front of a full house in Madison Square Garden. Later, I was touched by the cruelty of destiny which traps those who believe in it in the ruts of its doctrine, never letting them for a moment prepare themselves for their encounter with death. So, for the following chapters, I will retreat beneath the saving wings of nothingness, because there is nothing there which would give death a chance to knock you out. There, in nothingness, you already do not exist and you are at peace. But my time with Boba allowed me to relax, to admit a certain amount of reality in myself, and even to timidly accept the flow of time. What my father's strictness and the propaganda machinery did not manage to do was done by Boba's *elan vital*, by the warmth of his patriarchal heart. I have to admit that I relaxed: I drank quite a lot, I went to the movies, to boxing matches, and I even slept with some girls. Perhaps Providence itself removed Boba from the face of this world. God always does what is best for the individual, even though it does not always seem so to our narrow minds. That is the difference between God and the ideologists. For, if Boba had gone on living, I probably would have collapsed before the societal reality facing me and gotten a job working the switchboard of the Tractor Factory. Boba probably would have reached the ring at Madison Square Garden and been knocked out in the second round by Cassius Clay. We both would have lost.

My father met me once in the street. He was waiting for me, hiding in a doorway. He pretended to be surprised when he saw me. It must be admitted that he looked fine in his suit of powder blue English pinstripe material. With a haircut á la Tony Curtis. He even looked like Tony Curtis. Nothing unusual. At that time, he was incapable of anything else other than mimesis. Like all the others who had come from apes. It seemed to him that he had been absent from the novel for too long. He was afraid that he would be shrouded in a cloud of forgottenness. That is why he came looking for me. Pure vanity. There, in the time he belonged to, a fair amount of liberalization had occurred in the arts and it was no longer shameful to appear on the pages of dubious novels.

"*Well*," he said in English, "*Don't you think it's time to finish your stupid game?*"

Though he had changed his image, nothing inside him had changed. He wanted to impress me with his suit, his behavior, his knowledge of English. Especially with his knowledge of English. He was that stupid. Even parrots can learn English.

"*Stop bullshit me!*" I said, so that he could see that I had also mastered English. I had never studied languages. But the Holy Spirit spoke through me. He was also in the game. But my father could not understand that. At that time, he still could not understand.

"Is that any way to speak to your father?"

"I think the time has come for you to leave me alone. Why don't you just forget me? Why don't you just adopt a well-mannered boy?" I suggested.

"You are my flesh and blood," he said. Not without a certain amount of pride.

Whenever he used that argument, I felt like a cactus. Cacti grow from the bodies of their parents and then fall off. So, I quit talking about him and thus my father, at least for a time, ceased to exist. His new suit and haircut could not be of any help to him. I waited for him to grow distant, and then I started a chapter on Kowalsky.

13

I had just begun the chapter on Kowalsky when something terrible happened. Boba was murdered. No one had suspected anything beforehand: not I, not he, not his trainer, not the journalists, not even the police. The unknown killer simply carried out his plan, undisturbed. Boba was going to his training sessions, frying eggs, reading *Sports and the World*; I was writing about Kowalsky. From time to time, Boba would take the finished pages of the novel and read them. "Boring," he usually said. Only once, a day or two before he was murdered, he said: "I don't believe anyone is going to print your novel." Whether it was because my pride was hurt, or because my mom told me that she was making stuffed squash, or because of the intervention of Providence, I went home that day. When I returned to our room, I came upon a horrible sight. Boba was massacred, lying on top of a pile of magazines. They never found the perpetrator. But the investigation continues.

A crucial character in my spiritual life was a certain man named J. Kowalsky.

He wrote my first story, he gave me guidance in the secrets of religion, he proved to me that I did not exist and that I had been deceived by the propaganda.

I'll start with the story.

We wrote the story so that we could buy two bicycles. We divided up the work like this: he wrote twenty-eight pages of prose—that's how many pages were needed to buy two Rog bicycles—I signed them and took them to the editorial offices of the magazine called *Our Reality*. Neither Kowalsky nor I had literary ambitions. Later on I did have some, but I do not have them any more. At that time, it was 1949, things were different. I loved Gorky, Fadeyev, and my father. It was thought that the books of the first two represented reality adequately. We shall allow for that possibility as well. But what use do we have for reality? Although I was infinitely stupid, sometimes I would ask myself, "What about reality? We are only here temporarily. Thirty years ago, I was nothing. In thirty years, I will be nothing again. If reality is real, then I am not." But I stopped myself from talking about this out loud so that they would not be able to accuse me of Trotskyism, revisionism, nationalism, chauvinism, Parkinsonism, capitalism, and so on. No one will believe me: I went out with the voluntary work crews and toiled for up to twenty hours a day just so I could be real, just in order to construct myself. Ah, those days of renewal and construction, those years of enthusiasm in which there were no identity crises, when we firmly believed that we existed, when we believed it was GOOD for us if we abducted their women, and EVIL if they abducted our women. I was awarded medals three times as an outstanding volunteer. I have a photograph from that period: in it, my father and I are at the Adriatic Photo Studio. We are sitting at the table and behind us there is a screen with an image of the seashore. In the photograph, my father does not have a haircut á la Tony Curtis; on the contrary, his hair is cut like Stalin's. You'd never know that he was not actually sitting on the island of the seashore panorama mentioned above. I am sitting beside him, decorated in my worker's medals, grateful to my father for the flesh, the blood and the foodstuffs which made up my life. The scene would, doubtless, have made even Joseph Vissarionovich cry. That photograph is a significant document. I keep it in my files. As evidence that there is no difference between the seashore scene and the two of us. To the careful observer it is obvious that everything would soon fall apart. It was the time, as I said, of Fadeyev and Gorky.

And the story which Kowalsky and I wrote is heavily influenced by Fadeyev. He was our favorite writer. If I were to be perfectly honest, I would say that Kowalsky plagiarized the story under the heavy influence of Fadeyev. But the ends justify the

means. Bicycles were our goal, and you will see why. Thanks to
Fadeyev, we got our bicycles and we were very thankful to him. I
am still thankful to him. My father recently accused me of plagia-
rism. Someone from the Secret Police told him the details of the
story's origin. I did not feel guilty in the least. I do not know why.

The short story had an optimistic title—"The Time of New
Clocks." The editors all believed that the days of old, decaying,
Daliesque, imperialistic clocks were over. And we fit right in with
the trend. The action of the story takes place within a volunteer
work brigade: a girl from a bourgeois family has a beautiful ladies' watch, ornamented with diamonds. She is very proud of it.
She is secretly in love with a young man who teaches a course for
tractor drivers. Another girl is also in love with him, a girl from a
working-class family, hardworking and humble. The favor of the
lecturer for tractor drivers falls, at first, on the fashionable young
woman. This is where the climax of the action occurs: she fre-
quently takes furtive glances at her watch to see when the hands
overlap, hoping that the lecturer for tractor drivers is thinking of
her, and not of the girl from the working-class family. Someone
notices this and the brigade commander calls a meeting at which
he criticizes bourgeois mysticism. The lecturer for tractor drivers
realizes his mistake and lavishes his favor upon the hardworking,
humble girl, and he marries her soon thereafter and becomes a
father. The story ends with a speech by the brigade commander:

Comrades!

Soviet scientists are hard at work on a project for a new
socialist watch that will show, when the hands overlap,
the name of the person who the watch's owner is thinking of. In this way, all fortune-telling and sorcery will be
permanently eradicated. In the new society, it will have
to be known who is thinking of whom at all times.

DEATH TO FASCISM—FREEDOM TO THE PEOPLE!

All in all, quite a solid socialist-realist story. An excellent example of the genre. We could have made a career for ourselves. But we did not. I repeat: the bicycles were our goal. Nothing more. Certainly not this worldly fame. Besides, Kowalsky had decided to save my soul. It is true that my soul was worthless, but almost no one believed in the soul at that time, so every soul was welcome. More will be said about this in the appropriate chapter. Now, it is time for me to say something about my previous spiritual horizons. Apart from the fact that I was a prize-winning volunteer worker, I was also an idolater. I believed in Marduk. On my bookshelf, I kept a statue of this horned god, I would burn incense for it from time to time, I brought it sacrifices and decorated it with flowers. In the depths of my poor soul, I figured the following: god is god, even if he is nondescript, even if he does not exist. But if the scientific evidence turns out to be wrong, it is not bad to be in the good graces of some kind of god, even if it is Marduk, who is completely powerless within the boundaries of Europe.

One morning, Kowalsky and I got on our bikes and rode out of town. This was necessary for security reasons, I realized later. That is, my father was making a habit of eavesdropping on the events in the novel. We rode slowly beside each other. Kowalsky cast a backward glance to see if anyone was following us. Then he said:

"Listen, destroy that monster on your shelf. Believe in the true, invisible God."

I would do that for Kowalsky, I mean, I would have believed him. It is not hard to indoctrinate me, but it was just that he said God was invisible. That surpassed my powers of conceptualization. How could it be that I, who was visible and tangible, did not exist, and that the invisible God existed? I thought to myself, "That's not fair." It took me years and years to comprehend the logic of it. But Kowalsky was persistent. No wonder. The Holy Spirit was speaking through him, because in an age of overall atheism, the Spirit did not want to speak on its own behalf.

Kowalsky changed his tactics. He sped up as he tried to wear me down and soften me up.

"God is not invisible. That's what St. Gregory Palamas says. He is just too great and too small for us, the mediocre, to see him. *'Why doesn't God show Himself?'"* Kowalsky shouted, quoting Pascal. *"'Are you worthy of it?'*—*'Yes.'*—*'You are arrogant and therefore unworthy.'*—*'No.'*—*'You are unworthy of it that way too.'"*

Then he continued.

"It is better that way. God has shrouded Himself in His dark cloud. If He showed Himself in all His glory, everyone would believe in Him and they would turn the whole thing into a circus in no time at all. You know how it goes: delegations, congratulatory telegrams, and so on, and God doesn't like an uproar. And yet, all is not lost. You cannot hide from God anywhere. So, stop hiding in your *I* and God will find you. He is wherever you are. He is everywhere, even in you, under the condition that *you* are not in you."

Kowalsky was a gifted theologian. And an excellent cyclist. Those two things go hand in hand. He combined his two talents in order to lead me into the light of faith. He sped up even more. I was ready to believe in the whole thing if we could just stop and rest. I said, "I'm stupid, but isn't the Kingdom of Heaven prepared for such people, and for everyone else, if they just acknowledge it exists?" But then Kowalsky told me that the Day of Judgement was at hand and that the dead would rise, and I lost the little bit of faith that I had picked up on our outing. I almost fell off my bicycle.

"Wait, Kowalsky. Now you've gone too far. In the stories about light and darkness, about good and evil, about angels and demons, I could believe in such things. But this is too much."

"You are thinking about Marina too much to understand something like this," said Kowalsky.

And then he started laughing.

"Ah, Marina, Marina . . ." I thought.

14

Indeed, I was overdoing it a bit in my thoughts about Marina. I was in such a state that I would lie there for hours and just think about her. It was logically absurd, and chronologically too early for me to think about her, for at that time I still did not know if she even existed, but that is precisely why I was thinking about her. That is the real plot. Not like those plots that put a murder at the beginning of the novel, solve the crime at the end and thus take advantage of the readers' curiosity, forcing them to read hordes of nonsense in between. Somewhere, I believe it was under my bed, I had a flag. The top of it was blue with two golden crosses, the bottom was white—embroidered with big red letters which spelled out MARINA. On national holidays I would stick the flag out my window, and no one objected to it; the secret agents probably thought my house was the embassy of some kind of banana republic. The symbols of its heraldry are ultimately simple: blue is the color of nobility (and of Marina's eyes); the two golden crosses symbolize the clear light of Christ's first and second coming; white is the color of purity. One day, I cannot remember exactly when, I just sat down and made the flag, even though I had no idea who Marina was. And I will never find out; one should not expect any romance in this novel. But there is no doubt that I had seen her face somewhere. That is the only explanation for the fact that I can describe it with fair accuracy, which I will not do because of my aversion toward description. That is the only reason. And so, I imagined Marina on sunny slopes, wearing skis; at the seaside, on the beach; at her graduation party. I began asking myself how far my imagination could go. I thought about Marina for a long time, and only later did I understand that I would never see her, but by then it was already too late: by then, she was in my life and had no intention of leaving it, she neither could nor wanted to, since she had no idea about the whole thing. I know this is absurd. Zhdanov would be shaking his head. The lines about Marina are just too far from healthy reason. And that is good as well; that is the underlying meaning of my novel: *an exercise in the virtue of subordinating the willpower of human logic to the truth of things*, as one theologian wrote. I did not know this truth, nor do I know it now, I am waiting for it to reveal itself to me. It is important to slow down and then stop the thinking process. In that way many things can be learned. Otherwise, it is better to lie there and speculate about non-existent Marinas than to succumb to the error of thinking that you know something and that you can do something.

I often tried to stop this chaotic flow of thought which keeps me from remaining within myself, a flow which breaks away from me, aided by small tricks, and creates a relationship between things and people otherwise scattered in time and space, about which and about whom I must have some opinion whether I want to or not. Instead of existing, I think, I am unsure of my own self, I often ask myself who I am. The persistent results of my analysis are: a male, about thirty years of age, single, writing a novel, lying there thinking of Marina. That is the very nature of that sordid, endless thought process: always forced to go back to the beginning, but with the bitter knowledge that nothing has been thought through, that nothing has been clarified, that not a single outlet has been found. A man can never know more about himself than what could be uncovered by any investigating judge. However, even introspection into the depths, if something like that exists, does not produce better results: not a trace of identity anywhere, no sort of *I*, not even in the most impoverished form. There is simply not a single hook on which you could hang an accumulation of my hands, legs, eyes, intestines, memories, or thoughts, an impressive accumulation which, unfortunately, lacks structural support. Deep in our hearts, we all know that we do not exist, and yet everything just goes on normally. The world was made such that it is inhabited by real beings, which is completely absurd. No one in this world exists, and Marina is no exception. Our institutions are more real than we are ourselves, and in vain we try to fight for a place in the safety of their empires. It is impossible to utter a single word that is not a lie. If I meet an acquaintance on the street and I say "Good morning!"—I am lying. In fact I am saying, "I noticed you there, you exist." I could have said "Ping pong" or "Pyongyang," everyone knows that, but they return my greeting with the same lie "Good morning," by which they are saying that they also noticed me, that I also exist. That is etiquette, the rules of proper behavior in a society where people are gathered together only to lull each other into the illusion that they are alive, an illusion which is untenable in solitude. Once I read (in St. Augustine, I think) that God created two kinds of beings: one (the spiritual) is close to Himself; the other (physical) is close to nothing. I am convinced that this is the basic reason for the popularity of atheism: in proximity to God, nothingness is so obvious that it insults our vanity. Rarely does anyone make peace with the fact that they are nothing. Etiquette and other superficial forms are of no help here. Deep in our hearts we all know that God exists, it is just that no one dives down really deep, we all swim up on the surface. At the beginning of the 60s, a spectacular event occurred which was intended to push us even further from God—man flew into the cosmos. Gagarin announced to the more advanced portion of mankind that there was no kind of God up there, nothing except distant stars, emptiness and cold. Khrushchev was satisfied. My father as well. I watched a report about this miracle in a short propaganda film: Gagarin was laughing in the heavenly heights, by order of the Party, of course, because it was obvious that he was troubled and a little bit afraid.

There is no helping it, I thought to myself. You could even go to Saturn, and you won't exist there either.

15

"You're thinking about Marina again instead of listening to what I'm telling you," said Kowalsky.

He increased his speed rapidly. With great effort I managed to keep up with him.

"Now, I will tell you a story," he said. "It has been told many times. Yet, it isn't a waste of time if I tell it again. Whenever things are not clear to you, please stop me and ask for an explanation."

It was high noon. The sun was beating down on my brain. A perfect opportunity for a theological discussion.

"Almost two thousand years ago, in a stable in Bethlehem, the Son of God was born. Wise men from the East followed his star and came to him to worship him. At that time, Herod was ruling over Judea. He ordered that all the children, age two and under, be killed in the area of Bethlehem and its surroundings. But an angel led Jesus, with his father and mother, to Egypt. They returned only after Herod's death. They settled in Nazareth of Galilee, so that the prophesy would be fulfilled which said that the Savior would be a Nazarene."

It was not totally clear to me why the Son of God had to be born in a stable. Why should He have to flee from Herod? To be quite honest, I expected more from God.

"Until the age of thirty, Jesus worked in his father's carpenter shop. At that time, John had begun baptizing people in the Jordan. Jesus also went to get baptized. At first John didn't want to baptize him because he felt unworthy of doing so to the Son of God. Jesus told him that he would be doing the will of God, which is often mysterious to mortals. After his baptism, the Spirit led Jesus into the wilderness for Satan to tempt him. First, Jesus fasted. For forty days, he tasted no food, and after that he got hungry. Then Satan came to him and said, 'If you are the Son of God, make these stones into bread.' Jesus answered him and said, 'Man shall not live by bread alone, but by every word which proceeds from the mouth of God.'"

"I don't understand a thing," I had to admit.

"It is not as complicated as it seems," said Kowalsky. "Bread, that is the first temptation of every man. The stomach is a terrible tyrant. Hunger can be quite unpleasant. You wrote about that yourself in one of your dialogues with your father. In other words, the champions of secular ideas are, in fact, champions of their own gut. Courtiers do not throng in the halls of royal palaces out of love for the king, but out of their love for lamb chops and wine."

"And then?"

"Then Satan took Jesus into Jerusalem and placed him on top of the temple, telling him, 'If you are the Son of God, jump off, because it is written: *He will give his angels charge concerning you; and on their hands they will bear you up, lest your foot strike against a stone.*' Jesus overcame that temptation as well. Then Satan took Jesus to the top of a high mountain and showed him all the kingdoms of this world and their glory, and said, 'All these things will I give you, if you fall down and worship me.' Jesus refused. Do you know why?"

"No."

"Because Satan gives the kingdoms of this world to those who bow down to him. He gives them power and authority, the propaganda machinery and the police, the jails and the insane asylums. But Jesus' Kingdom is not of this world. Do you understand . . . ?"

"No," I said

Kowalsky increased the tempo.

"Do you know what the hardest thing for the Savior was?"

"No."

"The hardest thing was to convince the apostles of the necessity of his death."

"To be honest, that is the hardest for me to believe as well."

"To be honest, for me, too," Kowalsky admitted.

"Then why are you trying to convince me, if you yourself are not convinced?"

"Because it is absurd, Ananias, because it is absurd."

It's over, I thought. They will censor my novel. My father will rejoice. I will have to get a job working the switchboard at the Tractor Factory.

At that point the dialogue form ceased. I was running out of breath. The tempo was hellish. I will present the rest of the story in a condensed version, may I be forgiven on Judgement Day. So, Jesus knew he would be humiliated and crucified but he bore his burden. I could not get it into my head that God himself would allow such unpleasantness and humiliation. Fortunately, I never depended on my head too much, it was part of my father's flesh and blood, of his metaphysical slaughterhouse, I never lost sight of that fact, not for a moment. If anything ever saves me, that will save me. There are a couple of other things, actually, two straws on the vast open sea of doubt. Above all, if it is absurd that God is born in a stable, that he is humiliated and crucified, and if all of that really happened, then his resurrection also occurred, even though resurrection is a logically untenable idea. In the second place, it is undeniable that Jesus was an honest man, even if we do not get into the mysteries of incarnation, if we stick to his human nature. The Judeo-Roman establishment got rid of him to stay in power. I told Kowalsky that I doubted that Jesus would be crucified nowadays. The Americans would probably make big business out of the whole thing.

"You're deceiving yourself," Kowalsky said, "even today they would crucify him. I think he would get it even worse than on Golgotha, regardless of where he showed up. He would certainly be tormented longer; the methods of torture have improved since then. He would have to go through horrible torture. The Russians would accuse him of being an American spy. And vice-versa. To tell the truth—if he were God's Son—he would be exposed to even greater mockery than before. But the process of Jesus' crucifixion is an ongoing one. And all of us, in one way or another, are participating in it. On this side or the other. You are either crucifying Jesus, or you are being crucified with Him. *Tertium non datur.*"

At that very instant, Kowalsky picked up the pace again. I kept up with him for a time, and then, exhausted, I had to stop. Fighting to catch my breath, in the dim light of dusk, I watched how he rode off in a northwesterly direction, until he finally became just a dot shrouded in a small cloud of dust. In doing so, he wanted to remind me of the saying: *pulvis et umbra sumus*; that, from this world, we all depart in the form of a small cloud of dust.

I never saw Kowalsky again.

That day (I calculated it later) we covered 435 kilometers at a hellish pace, in a period of nine hours. This can be verified in the Guinness Book of World Records. The marketing people at the Rog Bicycle Factory always highlight this fact in their brochures and during special promotions.

16

I returned home firmly resolved to destroy my father once and for all, that vain creature, that clown who, despite all logic, enjoyed all the rights of a citizen, like millions of like-minded people worldwide. If he had had any honor, he would not have dared to be more than five inches tall; that was his real size. But intoxicated by his arrogance, without even the slightest right to be so, he was six feet three inches tall, he showed off his grand stature, he dressed it in fine suits of dark blue English material, he displayed it in public places. Once, during my meditations (I will write about them later), it was revealed to me (by the spirit) what the *spiritus movens* of such macho men, of such dialecticians is: namely, each of them has an enormous cunt inside them. That is why they decorate themselves with red ribbons, long sabers, pistols, and phallic objects of all kinds; in order to hide the truth, they pretend that they know the secrets of this world. But I saw through them, and they could no longer scare me; they were all between two and seven inches tall; homunculi-clitorises, insufficiently born, insufficiently alive, partial in all respects. Wretched and worthless. Because of that, they loved women so much, because of that they wrote their pulp poetry. Because like attracts like. Circumstances were just right for me. Somehow, somewhere, my father made a mess of something. Perhaps he had not known the date, maybe he had said something *today* which he should have said *tomorrow*, but—he fell from grace in the Party. His hair went grey overnight, but he still did not have any problems with his identity. He was a man of the old school. He continued to believe in life, historical determinism, work, glory, science, psychoanalysis, radiotherapy, volunteer fire brigades, art, progress, medicine, justice, and the flag. This is just a random selection from the list of nonsense he was willing to endorse, without any hesitation, at any given moment. He still believed that he had come from an ape; in that way he paid his dues to science. But if anyone called him an ape he was prepared to kill because his honor had been violated. Even with his last vestiges of strength he pretended to be hurt by the fact that I had left the College of Mining Geology and ended up in the nuthouse. From his point of view. In fact, my status in the nuthouse will never be clarified: was I locked up there, employed there, or did I just go there to visit someone else? Most probably all of that together, in the name of the unity of opposites. But my father's honor required that he worry about me, even though he grew shorter by a half and was only 3ft 1½ inches tall. Like most of his friends, he also identified with the title FATHER to such a degree that he slowly turned into a mannequin which held a pennant in its hand, stating I AM A FATHER. Such is the need for identity. Since inside, in his soul, he had nothing but a cunt, he had to search for an identity outside himself. He pretended to live, to work, to read, to have an opinion, to be happy or sad, all according to the needs of daily politics, but also in the hope that he would be rehabilitated within the Party. He was a shining example of what in psychology is called "a well-adapted person." Like any other father, you could have replaced him with a mannequin and no one would have ever noticed the difference, or one might even get the impression that an improvement had been made since—from a psychological point of view—mannequins are the most well-adapted persons. You can move them around, forbid them to write novels, convince them that they exist, lock them up—and they will never object in any way. In the end, my father did turn into a mannequin. That proved the Cabalistic claim, "Man, do not pretend that you're an apparition because you will become an apparition." But at that time no one would have guessed it. However, before he became a mannequin, my father became enlightened, he wrote a treatise called *The Metaphysical Coat of Arms of the Twentieth Century*; he traveled around America, and met several famous people. And yet, there was no saving him; he grew hard and turned into a doll, like the mannequins in the clothing store windows. Nemesis is merciless. But he did not know it then! He still hadn't discovered the cruelty of her kick. When he found out that I had made some progress with my novel, he almost suffered a nervous breakdown. His world began to disintegrate. That saved him from insanity: it was too late; the crash of his world falling into the abyss might have awakened the neighbors, so he pulled himself together in order to save a little bit of his family's reputation. The next day he came to talk to me. That day we acted out the first and last act of an absurd play entitled *Conversation of a Father and Son* or *The Conflict of the Generations*.

What is the daily family conversation but a trite farce? All you have to do is put a colon in front of the statements of the participants and you have a tragicomedy.

17

(A large room in our house. Necessary because of space, without which my father is unable to do anything. A wicker chair in one corner. My father in the chair. He is reading The Workers' Struggle. *In the center of the room is a large dinner table with six chairs. A wardrobe, dresser, and bookshelves.)*

FATHER (*thinking aloud*): It's eight years now that my idiot son refuses to understand that time is passing. When I think of the joy I felt on the day he was born, when I think of the hope I placed in him. I remember, like it was yesterday: a winter's day, I was pacing up and down in my office, I looked through the window and I saw the young workers' brigade chopping wood. It expressed reality so beautifully. And then about noon, Petrovski came in and said, "Comrade Corporal, you've got a son."

(At that moment, I enter the room. My father breaks off his monologue. He pretends to be reading The Workers' Struggle. *But he simply cannot keep quiet very long. After fifteen seconds, he puts the paper aside and addresses me.)*

FATHER: You are terminally ill. I don't see how it's possible for someone to have so much anger in them. Why did you write that I fell from grace? You've started using dirty tricks. Why did you have to go and do that?

SON: The ends justify the means. I wrote that you fell from grace because you are expected to. It will happen sooner or later. I have no choice. It's either you or me. You must understand. Either I will get a job at the switchboard of the Tractor Factory, or you will cease to exist and wise up. Our two worlds cannot hold together. You know that yourself. All authorities are corpses. They know that and that's why everything is all right for them if things just remain the same. In that way, they go on living in us somehow. It's not much of a life, but they are petty-minded and are thus satisfied with it. Fathers are cowards because they don't dare to die, and yet they have to die because that is the basic order of things—to make way for the following generations. What would your neighbors and friends say if you announced that you refuse to die. You, who are 80% your own father . . .

FATHER *(jumping on top of the wardrobe in anger)*: Don't you dare talk about my father like that, you derelict. I will disown you publicly. I'll take your inheritance away from you, I'll . . .

SON: Why don't you do it then? You won't. And I know why you won't. If you don't have a son, you're not a man. They will despise you. Just like they would despise you if you didn't have a house.

FATHER: Shame on you!

SON: I'm not ashamed of anything. We have simply made different choices. You want to die, I don't want to die.

FATHER *(calling to my mother angrily)*: He doesn't want to die! Can you imagine such a thing? He doesn't want to die. He's crazy. Absolutely crazy.

(Father jumps from the wardrobe to the dresser. He sighs. He has obviously decided to get angry. He is afraid of having a stroke, he's afraid of the very thought of death. From the way he is observing me, it is easy to see that, in his eyes, I am just a derelict who is avoiding one of the Holy Duties—death. He fails to understand that this is all just a novel.)

SON: This is just a novel.

FATHER: Just! Isn't that enough?

(This line he pronounces from under the bed. Strangely enough, it seems that he is not pretending. That he is really convinced of his words. But that does not keep him from acting like a madman, or from jumping from the wardrobe to the dresser, or from hiding under the bed. That is characteristic of all madmen: while talking about happiness, science, equality, and liberty they jump from wardrobes to bookshelves, and they are not even aware of it.)

FATHER: Tell me who this Heyse is. He has messed up your mind. Such nonsense would never cross your mind if you were by yourself. Tell me who Heyse is. I'll report him. He's headed for trouble.

SON: I don't know. I honestly don't know.

(My father leaves the room in protest.)

FATHER'S VOICE FROM THE HALLWAY: You'll never finish your novel. Never!

(I stand alone before the window, wondering what novel he is referring to. Through the window, in the distance, the smoke stacks of the Tractor Factory can be seen. Altogether, it expresses reality fairly adequately.)

18

The first signs that my family was falling apart were becoming evident. My mom was trying to halt its certain ruin, in vain. She hung pictures of our ancestors on the walls of all the rooms. Old ladies with moustaches and hunchbacked old men were staring at me with savage looks in their eyes because I refused to let them live on through me. All in vain. A family is a thing of flesh and blood, and flesh and blood are subject to spoilage, even market boys know that. The only thing that kept us together was our family lunches. My father kept shrinking; I almost felt pity for him, watching how he tortuously clambered up onto his chair. No one else even noticed it. Perhaps no one else dared notice it. Rather, it was probably because they were, indoctrinated as such, looking at him by inertia through eyes which were accustomed to him being six foot three. Once my grandma mentioned something about his height, incidentally, in a roundabout way, for she was incapable of hurting anyone. My father immediately pronounced her shortsighted and sent her to the doctor. So, my grandma, through no fault of her own, got some really thick glasses and was forced to wear them. For her own good, my father said. Under the heading GOOD, my father usually inserted only things which were good for him. This kept him under the illusion that he was a principled man, a creature who differentiated good and evil, which could not have been further from the truth. There are no such things as personality traits. Whenever someone talks about themselves, about their character traits, they are making it all up. They would only like for things to be that way. This became clear to me one evening when I was digging through my father's documents looking for something which would compromise him in the eyes of the reading public. To my amazement, among the birth certificates, marriage licenses, death certificates, sworn statements, falsified documents, deeds, receipts, promissory notes, and negotiable bonds, I found my father's contract with the Devil on a piece of yellowing paper. He saved even that among his documents. Quite in keeping with his mindless wish for existence, he cut deals with anyone who would guarantee him that the concepts on his list of utter nonsense were eternal truths. I do not doubt that he would have served in the Inquisition if he had lived two hundred years earlier. He loved documents, certificates and affidavits. He would have lost his mind if he had lost his identity card. That night, I found what I was looking for; the walls heard and saw everything, a contract with the Devil, I thought, should be a black enough spot on the record of a man who publicly interceded on behalf of eternal truths. I was anticipating my father's ultimate downfall, but then things went in a different direction altogether.

In those years a friend of mine was going through an extremely difficult identity crisis. Otherwise, he was a nice guy. He had a quarrel with his girlfriend and things started to go downhill. At times he felt as if he were dead, which was, metaphysically speaking, correct. But he could not come to terms with this. He had to attract the attention of those around him constantly, to make others notice him, because he believed in others more than he believed in himself. I mean in an existential sense. The first time he felt that he was falling apart, he lay down in the middle of the main street and began to moan in a muffled voice in order to arouse the sympathy of the passersby. A crowd of curious onlookers quickly gathered around him, but that hardly satisfied him. He did not begin to relax until two policemen arrived and began to beat him with their nightsticks because he was struggling and kicking. Only then was he sure that he existed because the police do not beat specters, they have their orders. Later on, when he was going through a crisis, my friend would start a fistfight: he would rush into a group of five or six strong young men, hit the first one he could, and the others would throw him to the ground

and beat him until they grew tired, to everyone's mutual relief.
But later on he enrolled at the university to study literature, he
began to go fishing, and things turned out all right. Not ontologically, we are too close to nothingness and we can do nothing
about it, but rather psychologically. He did not let it worry him
any longer. He brainwashed himself with Freud, understood that
it is man's fate not to exist and that one just has to live with it.
Later, he even dyed his hair and became a bon vivant. Only once
in a while would he fear death, just because he was supposed to,
for the sake of those around him, because society holds a certain amount of enmity for the brave; by its very nature, society is
a group of spineless idiots. I believe that is the basic reason why
one says only nice things about the dead. Not out of piety. There
is some truth in it. The only good man is a dead one.

19

A miracle happened after all. No one will ever know what caused my father to change his mind and realize that he did not exist. He hid his discovery for a long time. Maybe he was ashamed to admit that he had been wrong, maybe his pride kept him from repenting and publicly sprinkling his head with ashes.

Every afternoon he was still reading, or pretending to read, Darwin's *Origin of Species*. Too long had he believed that he came from an ape; he could not just give up on his memories, on his record, on the errors of his youth. But it was obvious that he no longer cared at all about evolution or paleontology. When he finally buckled under, he actually expanded the theory of man's originating from nothing. One can think poorly of him or not, but his enthusiasm is indisputable.

"It's true," he told me once, "man is created from nothing, but he cannot return to nothing. It is impossible to exist, but it is also impossible not to exist. Things have been oversimplified, they're too one-sided and polarized. Something is not quite right here."

Months passed before he made peace with the fact that he was nothing. Nothingness takes revenge on those who resist it in the most nefarious of ways, and the ways it took revenge on my father were nefarious indeed, even heinous. The world, which he had wanted to transform along with his comrades, now shoved him into a corner of the living room, into a wicker chair. He spent time there in complete resignation, while his pennant stating "I AM A FATHER" hung limply in his hand. Mom was constantly asking, "Well, where is your father?" even when he was sitting right there next to her, just a few feet away. My grandmother once walked right through him and did not even notice. Soon after, he was reprimanded and received his final warning before expulsion from the Party. His friends no longer came around. By himself, he didn't appear anywhere except in my novel, with no hope at all that the whole thing would at least be published. We were no longer father and son, but brothers, two creatures surrounded by a multitude of others who did not share our beliefs.

In spite of everything, I kept my distance because he continued to try and be a father, to be respectable, honorable, and strict. There is never complete honesty between two *I*s. Even when a man understands that he is nothing, he is still depraved because he is not completely nothing, at least that much is clear. My father was right: you can neither exist nor not exist. But our new common enemy was my mother. Even God Himself would not have been able to convince her that she was nothing, that the tangibility which she never questioned was nothing more than the simple imposition of just anything in the absence of something better. Since we have nowhere to hide, we carry our bodies around. Women are stubborn, and nothing could have ever been done about that. From early childhood, my mother believed in God, but she wanted to exist, and those two things are irreconcilable, because if you head in the direction of *to exist*, you thus distance yourself from God, as John Scotus Erigena has shown, if I am not mistaken. And when you exist, then you need new curtains, furniture, words, and the other things in which my father completely lost interest, to the overwhelming dissatisfaction of my grandmother and aunt. Once I heard my aunt, who had been against his marriage to my mother from the very beginning, telling my grandmother, "You see? First he was always out in the field, then he caroused with that bunch of reprobates, and now he doesn't exist." My grandmother waved her hand in disgust and said, "Forget it, everything will work out." She was a fatalist but, because she was old, they did not count that against her in the Central Committee.

Soon afterwards, my father found himself in the nuthouse. It is an unavoidable step on the way to enlightenment. I do not know what the reason was behind his appearance in the psychiatric ward. I saw him several times in a white lab coat. But that does not mean anything: you put on a lab coat and nobody questions you. It is a principle. You work on something or you pretend to be working on something, and realizing that you do not exist, you lose your will to finish what you have started. That is why people work: when you finish what you started, you get the impression that you exist. My father was crazy, they allowed him to wear the lab coat because of his former merits. He said whatever he wanted; that was the only way for him to get by the censors. All in all, he was only there temporarily, and he was not too bad off. We visited him on Thursdays and Sundays. We took him roasted chicken, he would giggle and gnaw on the drumsticks, hold my mom by the hand and sometimes he would say sadly:

"*Sic transit gloria mundi . . .*"

20

During those months I studied mysticism intensively. I shut my-self up in our large double-door wardrobe, which was part of my grandmother's dowry, and meditated. There was no doubt. I was a mystic. "A mystic is," Sartre writes, "a man who wishes to for-get something, his own *I*, the language which he speaks." Quite right. And yet, what kind of mystic was I? A caricature, a sketch, St. John of the Cross drawn by a clumsy child's hand. My esoteric efforts did not render a great deal. I never saw an unearthly light, I never felt that I was dissolving into the Absolute. Probably be-cause I had so many things to forget. Nothing especially impor-tant, a heap of lies and mistakes, but many such things had piled up; countless details were floating around in my head and I could not forget a single one. My excellent memory will be my undo-ing. I remember, for example, thousands of telephone numbers of which I have only used a few, and even those I will never use again. I hide this ability of mine so that they do not force me to get a job at the switchboard of the Tractor Factory and thus solve a social problem. Not only do I remember the phone numbers of acquaintances and friends, but I also remember the numbers of people whom I have never met in my life. I knew, for example, Marina's number. I did not know who Marina was, I will never know that, but I did know her number. If they exposed me to torture in order for me to tell them how I find such things out, even though I am a coward, I would not be able to tell them anything. That is the mystery: words are powerless, nothing true can be spoken; every sentence—regardless of how good the mo-tives behind it—is just a common lie. I wanted to call Marina once, to ask her who she was and why she never showed up, but I changed my mind. That is it—to call or not to call—that is the way my meditations floated around in my head while I was squatting in the wardrobe, in the heavy atmosphere there which was composed of: oxygen 15%, carbon-dioxide 20%, nitrogen 55%, naphthalene 10%. And that is not good. Because, as St. Bonaventure says: "A soul diffused with worries enters itself not with its own memory, with its hazy memories it does not return to the self with its own reason, enticed by desires it cannot return into itself in the desire for internal weakness and spiritual joy."

My soul, in whose existence I believed without reservation (despite the decrees to the contrary), was one of the most impoverished phenomena in both worlds, even though the soul is not a phenomenon. I admit this with a heavy heart, but it is impossible to deceive God. When I think about it more carefully, I did almost experience *satori* in a public toilet once; that was my mystical experience *par excellence*. Pure Zen: when you stop looking, you find what you were looking for. But I had no mystical experience whatsoever. Yet, one should be humble; that is the first rule of the mystic: be satisfied with the small, and then with the ever smaller. I always told myself that during my meditations in my grandmother's wardrobe. It is illogical and therefore good, it justifies my meditations about Marina, who I do not know. Is this not *agape*: to love with no use for it, to love without reason? The question is too hard. Striving for the impossible—that will be my undoing: I have always wanted to penetrate into the secrets of the universe, and I never even learned to tie my shoelaces before the age of thirty.

Once or twice the postman came and brought me something, first a postcard and then a letter, and that is all I can say about my correspondences. On the back of the postcard it said "Wishing you were here," signed "M." and on the front there was a Mediterranean motif with PALMA DE MALLORCA underneath. Who could that have been? Marina? No, impossible. There are limitations to the illogical. There was absolutely no way she could have known that I existed.

21

In the mid-60s my family began to disintegrate. My mother dedicated herself completely to her profession as a nurse, to the care of countless numbers of patients: elderly people and the young, birds, dogs, cats, dismembered dolls, dried flowers, tattered shirts. We moved into the hospital. My father objected, but my grandmother and aunt felt protected inside the hospital walls. This solution was the best for my father as well; his skin had grown hard and turned into pink caoutchouc. The doctors shook their heads suspiciously and whispered to one another in Latin.

From then on, the hospital was our home from which my mother—who had wandered too far in her research of pain— could not be thrown out, because they could not produce any kind of pension plan for her. Nor could they cite any single paragraph of the Associated Labor Act as a reason for her removal. On the other hand, that very same mother, the angel of hospital orderliness never understood my ambitions as a writer, and never understood literature at all. The only lessons she learned, in the fifteen minutes before sleep would overcome her, were from the New Testament.

"Son," she said once, as she was sterilizing some needles, "that nonsense will ruin you. Writers are to blame for Pilate's crucifixion of Jesus."

She turned a deaf ear to all my explanations that writers had changed over the last two thousand years. To make things worse, I was as healthy as a horse. I was never sick and I thus hauled another huge crate into the great warehouse of her disappointments. Because my mother's *civitas dei* was divided into two cities: the City of the Healthy and the City of the Sick. Her black-and-white ethic recognized only two categories of people: healthy

and sick. In her soteriology, there was only one path to salvation—disease. Outside the harmony of the City of the Sick—
that world with clearly established visiting hours, prescribed ther-
apies, and temperature measurements—the chaos of the City of
the Healthy ruled, in which anti-Christs, anarchists, thieves, and
robbers were on the rampage. In my state of pure health, she saw
the embryo of a dangerous heresy. My perfectly healthy blood
test results carried the stamp of Satanic arrogance and she was
ashamed of the roses in my cheeks when we were near her patients, like a teacher would be ashamed of his illiterate son in
front of the Minister of Education. For her I was a schismatic,
but she never gave up the hope that I would one day fall ill and
sink into the dim world of hospital solitude which impels one to
forgiveness and prayer.

"Jesus suffered great pain on the cross," my mother warned
me, carrying a basin of bloody bandages, angrily observing me
as I wrote page 187 of a poem about Marina, who would never appear. "The Lord was in great pain and you are bursting with
health. You go jogging, and whenever you get a headache you
take an aspirin."

But for my mom—contrary to the claims made in St. Augustine's *Civitas Dei*—the City of the Sick was not permanently
separated from the City of the Healthy. The possibility always
existed for a person to change their mind, to get sick and cross
the invisible boundary which divided the world of vice from the
world of disease. Thus my mother was secretly following Origen's
teachings, believing that, when everyone passed through purga-
tory in one of the departments of the General Hospital, apoca-
tastasis would be re-established. Her teachings were condemned
as heresy at the Ecumenical Councils of her colleagues, but she
was unwavering in her defense of her theology: the world is sick
and there are only sick people and those who hide their sickness
because they have been tricked by Satan (who is himself nothing other than a patient, a mentally ill schizophrenic). Just like a
madman who imagines that he is Napoleon, Satan imagines that
he is God. In order to heal the world, God became incarnate and

was crucified. In doing so, He took the whole burden on Himself, and through his resurrection he showed the path to salvation. That is why such great strides were being made in medicine. That is why the greatest sin was to feel good, to blossom with health, to have ruddy cheeks.

I could not understand her theodicy at that time. That was probably because I was still thinking logically; deconstruction was actually spreading. Everything was coming apart at the seams, at the premises, syllogisms, theses and antitheses—it was all going to hell, but I still had not figured out why it was better to feel bad rather than good, the wisdom of it escaped me. I was healthy, and therefore insensitive, although I flattered myself otherwise and used the alibi that I was a writer to appease my vanity. That was just an ordinary lie. It was my custom to move the patients who were lying on stretchers in the hallways out of my path with my foot (patients used to lie in the hallways in those days). I did this in order to be grander in the eyes of my fellow writers with whom I secretly entered our hospital / house at night to steal codeine, big yellow diazepams, and ampoules of morphine from the white metal cabinets. I did not do it because I was morbid by nature, although partly because of that, but because I was still partially indoctrinated. They had taught me all about drug abuse in biology classes.

"After death," they used to say, "a man becomes nothing. There is no other world." I figured it this way: if the dead are nothing, then why all the grieving? What good are memories? Pure logic, is it not? However, I did not dare say that to my mother; I retained a bit of respect after all. What interested me were Marina's eyes, big blue eyes which I would never see. At night, whenever there was a full moon, I would walk around and think about those eyes, forever lost. There were nights at that time in which I would sin prolifically. A fairly busy butcher shop could wrap months' worth of its goods in my poems about Marina's eyes. Her eyes were always around. At that time. But one should not doubt that afterwards they were, eventually, scattered to the four corners of the earth, that they went afar with dreams of happiness in those beautiful but somewhat dull irises of hers, that they went to see the deserted lands, landscapes, tarnished lies, towers and cities. Likewise, one should not doubt—I never doubted—that those eyes would one day be returned to the medical facilities of my mother's hallways, where, together with my eyes and those of my fellow writers, they would have time to understand that they were looking in the wrong direction, that what those eyes had been looking for was to be found on the other side of them, inside, in the depths from which their enthralling blue color was flowing outward in vain.

22

Then my father vanished. He crawled off somewhere on his stiff-
ened limbs. He did not even leave a message. At first, no one
even got excited about it. My mom put a mannequin wearing his
light blue suit in the wicker chair, she put a copy of *The Workers' Struggle* in its hand, and that was the end of the matter. Form
was being respected. Even the Central Committee did not object. I think I was nineteen at the time. At first I felt slightly uncomfortable, but then summer came around and I quickly forgot
the whole thing. My mother replaced the newspaper in the mannequin's hand every day, and the headlines created the illusion
of change in my father's face: it was obvious that something was
happening, the dates were changing, and thus one could con-
clude by deduction that time was moving on and that my father
was slowly aging. From the standpoint of socialist morale, everything was just fine: my father was not drinking, smoking, gam-
bling, or chasing women, and he was reading the Party press regularly. But I fell in with a bad crowd. I would come home late
at night. I did not miss my father. Anyway, the fathers of the
friends who I was hanging around with were almost exactly like
mine: each sat in his own corner, behind the newspaper, completely still, only now and then one of them would break wind
or belch just to be convincing (however, that is a matter of proper upbringing). Still, things could not go on like that indefinite-
ly. My mother knew that. Day by day the years would pass, the
time would come for my father to die, to make room for the new
generation; however, mannequins do not die and this could cause
a political scandal. The appearance of a single immortal would
shake the foundations of all the theories which say that man is
nothing after death. Probably because of that, more and more of-

ten people from the Central Committee were dropping by to inquire about my father's health. For the sake of the wider public, in fact, my mother said that he was suffering from an illness whose Latin name I have forgotten. I only know that it manifested itself through complete stiffness. This was a clever move by my mom. She must have loved my father secretly, although she never wanted to admit it. For if you presuppose *a priori* that a man has no soul and if he is sitting there unmoving, you should go figure out if he is dead or not, if he is a mannequin or the real thing! To create an illusion of liveliness, my mother tried a variety of tricks. Ever more often, my father would be holding *The Communist*, and in the afternoons it would be *Herr Eugen Dühring's Revolution in Science*, or *Capital*. But the tension continued to rise. Around town, it was rumored that my father had emigrated to America, which could very well have been true. I have already said that my father was capable of anything. But for a while, things went on as always. Besides the usual pennant "I AM A FATHER," my mother put other small pennants in his hands, saying "DID YOU MEET MARINA? YES—NO," or "ARE YOU EVER GOING TO FINISH COLLEGE? YES—NO." These sentences were intended for me. I would circle "NO" and thus some form of communication between the two of us was taking place. Observing my father, my aunt said, "One shouldn't get involved in politics." My grandmother added, "A married man must think of his family first." My mom enrolled as a part-time student of medicine. All night long she would study anatomy, Latin declinations and *consecutio temporum*. Just before dawn she would secretly study the writings of Bombastus Paracelsus.

23

One morning, my father reappeared just as mysteriously as he had disappeared. And he was not alone. With him was an honest to goodness, real live black woman. "This is Mary Sue," my father said. My grandmother crossed herself with both hands and whispered, "Lord preserve us and all the saints." My aunt went to her room in protest.

"Where have you been? Did you know that they've expelled you from the Party?" my mother shouted.

It was obvious that she was disappointed because he did not come home penitently, or sick, but rather in top form, with a suntan.

"Expelled, you say?" my father said. "I couldn't care less."

He started unpacking his suitcases. "Scoundrel!" shouted my aunt through the door of her room, which she had left ajar. At that moment, I came in. My father looked at me, put a Chuck Berry record on the stereo, and told my mom and Mary Sue, "*Go now, girls*" in English. We were left by ourselves. My father beckoned to me and handed me a pair of Levi's. "These are for you." Then he proudly unpacked his travel guides, plane tickets, stickers from luxurious hotels and a multitude of photographs. In one color photograph, under an enormous palm tree, I saw my father with Tony Curtis. They were standing there with their arms draped over each other's shoulders, in their bathing suits, smiling at the camera. "That's for you, too," my father said. "Turn it over." On the back, in purple ink, it said, "To my friend's son! Tony."

"Shall we go fishing on Sunday?" I asked.

"Of course," my father said. He threw the mannequin out of the chair, flopped down in it and started paging through *The Workers' Struggle*.

My aunt was peeking around her door. In the kitchen, giggling and chatting in a language unknown to me, my mom and Mary Sue were making blackberry juice.

24

My grandmother died soon afterwards. We only noticed it a couple of weeks later, when it started to get warm, and that is a perfect illustration of the stage of disintegration my family had reached, of how steeped each of us was in the depths of our own selfish obsessions. My mom actually cried at the funeral, together with Mary Sue, because even mothers and blacks are still not as tough as we Europeans. After the funeral, I locked myself in my room and played the blues. That same day, in the evening, my father asked me to come see him in his room. He took a monograph in English from the shelf and showed it to me. "I became a celebrated author in the States with this," he explained. "It is my life's work, *The Metaphysical Coat of Arms of the Twentieth Century.*"

The coat of arms was based on an inverted pentagram, with the top point sticking in the emblem of the UN. In the upper left point of the star were pictures of Agatha Christie and Sigmund Freud, in the upper right was the figure of Adolph Hitler at a podium in front of a vast ocean of people wearing helmets and carrying banners which said "WORK, ORDER, PEACE." In the lower left point of the star, the following symbols could be seen: a man kneeling down to fix an automobile, a dancer from the Crazy Horse cabaret in Paris and a TV set. In the center of the star was a crucifix. In the lower right point, under a Seiko advertisement, were portraits of the great ideologists of the nineteenth and twentieth centuries, and in the vertical point of the star, the one stuck in the UN emblem, was the saying "ERITIS SICUT DEI."

"And you got famous for this?" I asked dubiously.

My father did not reveal that he was hurt by my lack of faith in any way. He checked to see if anyone was standing behind the door, he plugged up the ears in the walls, sat down in his chair and began to interpret his metaphysical heraldry for me.

"I think you're mature enough to understand a few things," he said. "The symbols in this coat of arms are not there by accident. We'll go from top to bottom. From left to right. The first thing you see is the figure of Agatha Christie, though that's not the right place for her, Freud should go there, but I gave her priority because she is a woman. The disintegration of our family, the disintegration of values in general, begins with the work of that great Viennese psychiatrist, that arch-coward, that weakling of all weaklings. Freud was a real hedonist. I have nothing against that, I myself am a hedonist, but Freud constructed a wicked theory in order to justify his hedonism to his own conscience and to the conscience of Europe. In stating the scientific assumptions of his theory of psychoanalysis, he showed hedonism to be natural and necessary, which is not true. It is a matter of choice, and it is a faulty choice at that, because enjoyment and luxury soften a man up, make him too weak to resist the elements. One who has grown used to enjoyment will agree to anything just to enjoy himself; he will participate in the foulest of games in order not to go hungry, in order to get a discarded piece of bread. Freud feared death like the plague throughout his life; that is a generally known fact. And that is also evidence of his guilty conscience. Fear of death is the presence of death, death *eo ipso* . . ."

"And Agatha Christie?" I asked. "What does Agatha Christie have to do with it all?"

"That's her place," my father went on. "That lady dedicated her life to the possibility of committing the perfect crime. That's how far the desire for perfection has sunk; to search for perfection in lawlessness. Now we come to the right point of the star. In it Hitler stands before a mass of uniformed people who are carrying the slogans "WORK, ORDER, PEACE." That is Freud's spiritual heritage: people who are obsessed with enjoyment, focused on the minute interests of their own families are not *people* at all. They are the atoms of an amorphous mass. Hitler came to power at a time of crisis and he offered bread. The majority traded their freedom, their humanity for food . . ."

"I don't get it," I pretended to be confused.

"Don't worry," my father said. "One day you'll understand that when you trade your humanity for food, you become a beast."

Then he continued.

"We move now to the lower left point of the star. This man who is kneeling down, don't you see anything strange there? Nothing strange, at first glance. But perhaps that fellow is the slave-driving owner of a cannery, perhaps he is an arrogant politician, kneeling before the creation of human hands; he is bowing down to his idol, just as they used to bow before Baal. Idols are located down here on earth; they attract our attention so that no one looks to the heavens any more. At the same time, in the lower right point of the star, the ideologists are talking, constructing their theories, arguing their points, and time is moving on, which is indicated by the Seiko advertisement . . ."

"And now," said my father after a meaningful silence, "now look at the coat of arms as a whole. It is based on an inverted pentagram, the symbol of Satan, which circumscribes the contours of a goat's head. On the odd point, the goat's beard, the statement "ERITIS SICUT DEI" stands. Those are the words the Serpent used to deceive Eve in the Garden of Eden. They mean "YOU SHALL BE LIKE GODS." All of history is just a series of unsuccessful attempts by humans to become like gods. In our effort, we have ceased to be humans and have become mannequins. But all is not lost; the entire coat of arms is only a reflection in a looking glass. In it everything is upside down, everything is backwards. Did you notice that in the center of the pentagram is Christ's crucifixion, a tiny cross, a crack in the looking glass . . ."

25

The process of my family's disintegration was steadily headed toward its point of departure. First, Mary Sue took off with some sort of jazz band. We never heard from her again. My father was inconsolable. He allegedly went to Syria to study apocryphal documents about the coming of the Antichrist. He was funded by an English foundation, and there we lost all trace of him, at least temporarily. My aunt packed her bags and moved to England, where she got a job as a fitter in a department store for the well-to-do. She sent us a postcard from Cardiff Forest, and then a letter from Bradford. Included with the letter was a picture: she was standing with Mary Stuart in a wax museum. Mom left her medical studies, put the mannequin back in my father's chair, shoved the newspaper *Politics* into the mannequin's hands, opened the door on the warehouse of her disappointments, received a shipment of heavy crates, signed the bill of lading, and went back to her patients. She thought of retiring from time to time, of the long days ahead when she could write down her patho-eschatological visions.

I have to admit that she has been much kinder to me recently, because I have contracted *ulcus bulbi duodeni* and *bronchytis chr*. This raised my reputation in her eyes to a level which I could never have dreamed of. Personally, I think that the disintegration of my family was a good thing, much better than the trite farce "The Idyllic Family" which we had been acting out for so long. Anyway, it is a natural law: anything made of pieces necessarily falls apart. I believe my father would formulate it that way. Recently he was reinstated in the Party, and a farmer's cooperative in some remote village was given his name. Formally, he is still among us, in his chair. I dropped by to see him yesterday. Like always, he was reading *The Evening News*. I looked at the headline.

It carried the date June 6, 1968.

Vanishing Tales

Introduction to Schizophrenia

I didn't want my mom to think about me a lot. It felt awful inside the grey matter of her cerebrum, completely preoccupied with virtues or with incorrigible vices, depending on her mood. I felt surrounded by a shame of unknown origins which not even Sigmund Freud (who was incidentally present due to the fact that I had just read *An Introduction to Psychoanalysis*) could have said anything definite about. My mom was constantly dreaming that I would become a doctor, a surgeon, and she often imagined me preforming complicated operations, never even considering my fear of blood and my disgust toward flesh. The only useful thing that came out of the whole ordeal was that I learned Latin really well, and I used this knowledge whenever I wanted to be incomprehensible even to myself. But that wasn't all my mother did; somewhere in her frontal lobe, where crazy ideas, people from her memories, Bulgarian lieutenants shot in the side of their heads, *and worse*, appeared, she also ran a bar, a *divé*. In any case, the *divé* did not make a significant income. My mom kept it running not so much because of the profit, but rather to maintain the illusion of doing something useful. At the time, she was already good for nothing, not even a meal. Driven by her self—or rather—by her madness, by the former rational mother who wanted to overcome her schizoid twin, she had become lost in the complicated account books of imaginary debts. I think that was a clever move. My mom would never have crossed the threshold of such a dubious joint—even in her maddest state—and yet her memories dropped by regularly and I was also spending most of my time there in vain attempts to lose my own mind. If I felt terrible in my own thoughts, inside my mother's I felt *terrible* or even **TERRIBLE.** I simulated madness so that I wouldn't

be distinguished from my surroundings, vacillating between reality and hallucinations, and when I grew bored of it all I would
crawl through my mom's optical nerve to her center of vision and
observe her reflections of the external world. Sometimes I would
catch sight of a girl and I would want her to see me as well, but
that wasn't possible: no matter how hard someone stared into my
mom's pupils, they could see nothing except the characteristic
dullness of the eyes of the mentally ill. This sentence was later
scratched out, then written in again in order to emphasize the im-
possibility of contact between what is *INTRA* and what is *EXTRA*:
no matter how hard someone stared into my mom's pupils, they
could see nothing except the characteristic dullness of the eyes
of the mentally ill, period. For a long time I thought about leaving it out of the final text after all. My friend, M. Knežević, or
Calcium Sandoz, it makes no difference, said that this dilemma
made no sense, that all of those things were just reflections, electric impulses, the movement of energy and that we exist because
of THAT, and THAT exists not because of us. But why do we exist? I got the Zen answer: *And that exists not because of us.* In fact,
I got nothing. It was just electric impulses . . .

In the meantime, my father had gone bad and we'd had to
throw him out. The past perfect tense existed. I understood
somehow that this shouldn't bother me. When something happens and becomes the past that does not mean that it is finished
once and for all. It continues to happen *in reverse*; it becomes the
past of the past and so on to the end, which is the repeated beginning. I climbed up to the third floor and then descended backwards, again finding myself on the ground floor. I thus proved everything I was saying. Detonations were reverberating all around:
BOOOOOM! BOOOOOM! BOOOOOM! My mom was burst-
ing with good health. I could easily tell the difference between
bursting with good health and bursting with anger. Bursting with
health is a series of sharp cracks. Almost like a salvo. I used to hit
her when she did that but as I grew closer to madness I understood more and more that she was working so that I could finish
the medical studies that I didn't even intend to enroll in, and that

from dawn until ten in the evening—when bars are required to close by law—she was slaving away for my own good and pretending to burst with good health so that no one would get the idea that she was ill, because that might turn away the customers who were already a rarity. But my mom was losing her mind incomparably quicker than I was and she did not realize that I was going crazy as well—compared to her I seemed sane—and that I would never graduate from college. She forgot about me for a moment so I took the opportunity and went home. There, glasses were falling from the table to the floor where certain death awaited them, the cabinet was creaking, the chairs were barking, the door was opening and closing by itself. There are various interpretations of such phenomena, but I know for certain that they are the psychoses of furniture. All of those objects had suffered more than any man could have survived. The worst off was the cabinet. Incurable schizophrenia. Its personality was splitting into two independent dressers. I put some Nozinan tablets in its drawers, but in vain. After all, there is a difference between the human psyche and the psyche of inanimate objects.

The chairs were, as I said, barking, trying to break their leashes, and they certainly would have succeeded if those leashes hadn't just been assumptions. I know that chairs usually don't bark, but I was so absentminded, so forgetful that, there you have it—it so happened that I forgot that chairs don't bark. Dogs have four legs and chairs have four legs. Since I was paying no attention to logic, that analogy was enough for the chairs to start barking. I know that chairs don't bark otherwise, but I had justification; I could draw a parallel: four legs—chairs—dogs—psychosis. Yes, in the final analysis, psychosis. I imagined some even stronger leashes, grabbed onto a series of clear memories and went outside. In the moments when my thoughts were forced into the shape of the city bus schedule (which had to happen occasionally because it is impossible to retain an awareness of one's own existence all the time), and when I had to make peace with my existence as a temporarily indisputable fact, I would pretend that I was not myself but someone, anyone, else. That was the only way I could walk down the street. All eyes were turned to me and all lips were whispering: that's the guy whose chairs keep barking. I was going somewhere that I didn't want to go when I suddenly saw a girl. I didn't know her, but I couldn't remember where it was that I didn't know her from. She definitely indicated that she liked *him*. It took me a good hundred yards to realize that *he* was ultimately me. I turned around and went back but now there was another problem. There were other girls that I didn't know in the same spot and I only barely recognized the right one by the fact that I didn't know her in an intimate sort of way. Things got even more complicated: I couldn't remember the details of what *the guy* looked like. So I pretended that I was someone else, **someone else**, SOMEONE ELSE, and even **SOMEONE ELSE**, but she wanted *someone else*, semi-colon; somehow we concurred in the end and agreed to meet up at 5:00, later that day. I immediately went to the *divé* because it coincidentally rhymed with *that day*. At the *divé*, M. Knežević or *Calcium Sandoz*, whichever, and a certain G.V.F.X. were sitting around. This meant they were half-drunk, which surprised me a lot: M. Knežević never drank because he had a degree in French language and literature. Straightaway I announced to them that I was renouncing madness, that I intended to get married, finish my medical studies, get a job, have several children and live long and happily; only, after some time of course, to grow disappointed, start drinking in secret, and no period This did not surprise them. They had already read in *the New York Times* that I was a characterless bum. My mom was insisting that I move out on my own as soon as possible, but I didn't take her seriously. That particular day, time was flowing terribly slowly. One drop every six hours. Somehow I made it to 4:30 and then, because of some unjustifiably urgent business, I was twenty minutes late for our date. I really did want to meet up with her, so I turned the hands on the clock back half an hour and waited. She didn't show up at five. I waited a few more minutes for her and then I left, firmly resolved that I would never forgive her. I went back to the *divé* to bring *this* chapter to an end. My pencils were awfully dull, and I had the uncom-

fortable feeling that I had gone off-topic. M. Knežević comforted me, "Don't be so sad! *Women* is just a collective noun. Take it
purely grammatically." *What was he talking about?* I started thinking in English, but since most of the people there had a com-
mand of the language I switched to Ancient Egyptian and tried
to retrace the story of what hadn't happened. I hadn't met the girl
in reality, but in the sphere of supposition we went on with our
grey lives as citizens of a developing country.

G.V.F.X. claimed that I was sure to become a philosopher. I
didn't know whether I should believe him because he was tipsy.
My mom objected: "First he has to graduate from college. *Primum
vivere deinde filosofari.*" I closed my eyes to make her vanish, but
she turned on the light and so it started to get dark outside. Better
not to talk about that. I went home, fed the chairs, intentionally got lost, looked for myself and shouted, "Where are you, you I
AM, where are you, you son-of-a-bitch," and in the end I died of
boredom. For a long time I thought about whether it makes any
sense to go on writing after death by boredom. M. Knežević asked
me, not without maliciousness, why I was writing at all. Suddenly I started thinking, feverishly thinking, in Sanskrit so that I
wouldn't understand what he was saying, "No matter how much
you lie to yourself, saying that you're writing because of this or
that, you're only writing to forget yourself." Was he right? I don't
know. I didn't understand a word of anything he was telling me.
Anyway, we were at the *divé*, and my mom is the only person who
is ever allowed to be right at the *divé*. Then, into the *divé* walked
two attractive women and M. Knežević started shaking, trembling because—in spite of his college education—he had a weakness for women. In those instances, he reminded me of *Calcium
carbonate*, but that similarity was purely formal, frivolous even.

"Bulshit," said Knežević because he didn't speak English.
"Something must exist, some Absolute. There must be Someone
who forgives us for everything, who will look beyond all of our
obscenities." He spoke just to impress the ladies. He could not
have known that I had already outlined everything in detail for the
second chapter and that as soon as my mother's mind wandered

to something else the chapter would end and everything would go to hell. Anti-psychiatry contends that sexual activity is an excellent therapeutic treatment. And yet, it's much easier to make plans than to carry them out. The central feature of plans is that they are never carried out. M. Knežević introduced me as an author. "You haven't read his *Vanishing Tales?*" he asked them. Naturally they hadn't read it because those stories still had not been written, therefore they also could not vanish, and even if they had been written and had vanished, the two of them would never have read them because they only read cheap romance novels, if those girls existed at all, that is: if they weren't just narrative fiction. Who can be sure about that? Who can be sure about anything, and especially of the reality of two, truly beautiful, but questionable female apparitions in my mom's *divé*? Again, I wondered: Why am I writing? That activity has only gotten me into trouble. But it is what it isn't, and once again, period. And I also, indeed, like women. They are quite bearable if they are properly prepared. Even though my handwriting was illegible, M. read my thoughts. It wasn't difficult for him because he had graduated in French and worked as a theater director. "*Cannibal ante portas,*" he said. Whatever the case, we took our clothes off, began screaming and chasing each other about, and then suddenly the door opened and, as if in a story, into the *divé* came a dozen or so photojournalists from the yellow press. Flashes went off all around us and we were captured in faded pornographic black-and-white photographs, in poses unfit to mention in a serious book of stories, even if those stories vanish at the end of everything they have to tell.

"Scheise," said M. Knežević because he didn't speak German. "We really could have done without this. What will my wife say if she accidentally sees the photos somewhere?"

That very instant I began thinking in Etruscan so that I could increase the alienation between myself and the lusting creatures who were observing me like investigators. There is a photograph from the Interpol files which got lost in time, it disappeared in the overall vanishing of things. I can say only that it showed the face of a character with a vacant, maniacal stare. Once it had been enough to look at that photograph and understand my decision to ultimately break away from that character. Now, there is even less evidence because in the meantime many things have vanished, and so in this sentence I feel like Proust in *In Search of Lost Time*. I had to break away from him (author's note: from *me*) because, between us, all that remained of him was an obsessive persecution complex and who knows how bad it would have gotten if my mom hadn't started remembering intimate details from her youth and, polite person that I am, I discretely slipped out of the *divé*, stood in the middle of the street, and got swallowed up by the earth out of shame.

I found myself in some other street. I walked along because I was supposed to and who knows where I would have ended up if I hadn't come across a barrier in front of a construction site with the warning: PEDESTRIANS CROSS TO THE OTHER SIDE!

I crossed to the other side, angry because there was no comma after PEDESTRIANS. I still didn't know where to go, but the change in direction had introduced a small change in my movement toward the indefinite direction of *anywhere but here*. In truth, I could have hopped over the barrier, but I would have exposed myself to the danger that a construction engineer with a naked girl in his arms might fall on my bare head. A few months later—when everything had already irrevocably vanished—M. Knežević—*Sandoz*—asked me what I wanted to say with that sentence. It was then that I told him this story which is, I admit, very difficult to believe: It is not logical that construction engineers should fall out of the clear blue sky just like that. The falling of engineers depends on a confluence of many sad circumstances. It is a well-known fact that the college of engineering is exceptionally difficult and that students are forced to study a lot if they want to finish their exams on time. Since they spend a lot of time at lectures, workshops and studying, they don't have time to have fun with girls. This creates a wound that never heals in their souls, darkened and tormented by the blueprints of grey skyscrapers. When they graduate and get jobs, they have much

more time, although I personally think that they have much less
time because their best times have vanished irrevocably. But let's
say that they have more time. Construction engineers use their
free time to wait for young girls in the dark streets of the new
parts of town, ostensibly to teach them about the fatigue of mate-
rials. Young girls are not so naïve. They hide in unfinished buildings, places where construction engineers feel at home. Their hiding shouldn't be taken seriously; it's a part of a well-known game
which leads to a chase along the scaffoldings. Construction engineers are heavy, and it often happens that a board will break.
Then they fall to the street below, but not without a young girl
in their embrace. If it happens that they accidentally kill a random pedestrian, they bear no liability because on the barriers
around all construction sites it is clearly written: PEDESTRIANS
CROSS TO THE OTHER SIDE! even though there is almost
never a comma after PEDESTRIANS.

"Merd," commented M. Knežević because he didn't speak
French.

And then I saw *something like a thread*. It appeared to lead
off in a particular direction. That *something like a thread* was just
a simile. I know that now, but I did not at the time. Anyway, it
was insignificant. I followed IT and wondered why the language
I speak is teeming with the words IT and THAT? In the meantime, the thread led me to an apartment where *the girl* was waiting, along with a few people including a man whose breath contained an inordinate number of tuberculosis bacteria but who
otherwise looked quite decent. For the sake of general security,
I conjured up a bunch of Young Alexander Flemings and a multitude of small Penicillin laboratories. But what about *her*? She
had changed terribly after just a few pages. She looked like Beckett and she was missing her left leg. She was attempting to produce the impression that it just seemed like her leg was missing,
but it could clearly be seen that she had no left leg and question
mark? What happened to her leg? I didn't dare to ask. But now
that I think about it a little more, it wasn't quite that simple. She
had a prosthesis. Her leg extended down to approximately LE_,

and in the empty space was filled with an artificial wooden limb. It would be best if I present this visually:

Verbal Transcendental Portrait

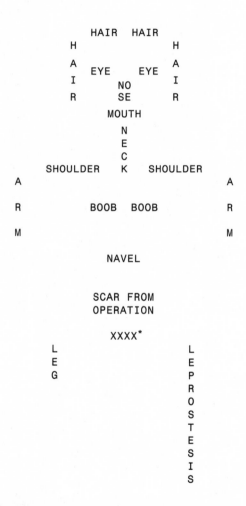

That's it? She said to me, "Klümm!" What do you mean, *klum*? I asked, but she shook her head and corrected me, "No, not *klum*!

---

* Self-censored

Klümm!" I didn't see the difference whatsoever. I didn't know that language. It almost certainly meant something stupid. I wanted to be alone for a while, so I went to my room. There was no doubt that I would soon lose my mind. I identified completely with the typewriter and I wrote the word *solitude* so many times that I finally wore out the ribbon. Then I got tired and the room was quadrangular or maybe it only seemed to be. Now that I think about it, the room was not quadrangular. The walls formed a barely perceivable octagon of an irregular shape. Groping around and bumping into objects, I looked for the bed which was not in its usual place but in quite a different one, and the possibility existed that there was no bed in the room at all so, tormented by the length of the sentence, I decided to sleep vertically, but sleep simply could not get used to that position. The chairs were barking so loudly that I thought they had gone rabid. I had to pretend that I was someone else.

Around midnight, Radio Belgrade announced that I had won the 1979 Nobel Prize for Solitude.

Recognition always arrives too late.

I wrote a letter to the Swedish Academy in which I politely refused to accept the award, and suddenly I began to vanish uncontrollably, to disappeaaaaaaaaaaAAAAAAAAAAAAA

The Drawing

In my hand there is a pencil, in front of me is a piece of paper. I'm supposed to write stories that will vanish. A fairly difficult assignment. I just can't get started. I draw a couple of lines, some sort of circle and there you have it—circle by circle, line by line and a face grins at me and says: "Hi, Bas!"

And I, how silly, begin conversing with a childish drawing, with a really amateurish drawing. Moreover, an impossibly talking drawing. "Hi, drawing," I say, "there must be some sort of misunderstanding."

The face frowns.

"What do you mean misunderstanding? I say 'hi', and you say there's some sort of misunderstanding. Don't you believe that drawings can talk?"

Then his expression changes. He becomes mocking.

"Listen, drawing, I have a big job ahead of me. I have to write a lot of stories and I really don't have time to talk with you."

"Here's what I think of your stories."

He's mocking me. I have sunk so low that childish drawings are mocking me. Well, that just can't be, I think. I know how to deal with this.

"You know what," I say, "now I'm going to close my eyes and when I open them you will start to vanish. You'll vanish, and you won't be anywhere."

That's the way one should deal with drawings. The face grew really worried.

"Don't do this to me," it said, barely audible.

I have nothing against drawings, but I have work to do and I cannot allow myself to put it off, wasting time arguing with a childish drawing. So, I close my eyes, open them—and look: the eyebrows are gone.

I close my eyes again, open them. The nose is also gone.

But the mouth is still there. I forgot about that. It's still talking. "All right! This time you win, but you should know: sooner or later you, too, will vanish, just like that."

I need to finish it off as quickly as possible. It talks too much.

I rub my eyes and—sure enough!—that babbling mouth is gone.

All that's left is a phantom, a ghost. The rest happens by itself. First one eye disappears.

And then all the rest. It's a fairly horrible sight, the vanishing of a scribble which is on one side illuminated by a dull light, and on the other side covered with shadow. It turns into:

And that's all.

Surroundings

Alone, surrounded by nothingness, in a room without a past or a present. On the right is a window, on the left, a desk and several books. Those are assumptions. Behind them, nothing exists. Everything I see is indeed a completed projection which I made up just so I would have a room in which to die. Where I will suffer. It is no one's fault! In any case, how many of them, like me, are languishing in unbearable conditions, how many of them are being approached by death, and how many of them don't exist at all. Countless non-existing, countless impossible creatures are peering through the window. I exist too little to pay attention to phantoms, I exist too much to take into consideration that which really is. It is enough for me to close my eyes and the projection fades into the surrounding nothingness. Deceived! Life is such a relative concept. As opposed to death! I touch my body, I stick pins in my hands, I slam my head into the wall, and in doing so I prove nothing except that touch and pain exist. It is impossible to prove me. No matter how discouraging that is—THAT is not me. And so for me not to be me, for me in the end to die with the bitter feeling that I've been deceived, I had to be born, and for me to be born the person who gave birth to me had to be born, and for her to be born, a man had to die in a war, and generally speaking, so many things had to happen for the sake of something so fragile, nonsensical and painful as my existence in a room without a past or reality in which time passes so slowly in relation to other rooms so that what I am saying—I'm not even saying it yet. That is the distant future. I doubt I will experience it in the so-called real world, where death is just the ultimate consequence of a series of previous deaths. I, a personal pronoun in the first person singular; raped before birth in the uterus of a mother, deceived, left to the mercy and cruelty of the unforesee-able flow of thoughts and reason which find a thousand justifica-tions against suicide. And nothing happens. Two negations are an affirmation—I read that in one of the books—and *nothing* ulti-mately happens. What could possibly happen before death? and what can I say, at all, about myself? and am I saying THAT at all or is THAT talking to me? and why am I talking at all? I have no other choice: I must speak. I must just say anything, because everything I say slips away and vanishes and—I must constantly think of huge blocks of marble, imagine vast steel plates so that in the all-encompassing chaos of inconstancy I might grasp a few straws of the illusion of solid and lasting objects, for which I can desperately grasp as I go under the surface.

Language Class Essay on the Topic of "Insomnia"

That night I could not fall asleep no matter what. I went outside, into the rainy street, and walked a long time; the wind refreshed me, so I went back and then a misunderstanding occurred: Without turning on the light I lay down, but there was already someone lying in the bed. Someone of the female gender. I sensed it with my sense of smell. Now what's done is done. We were lying in the dark. Somewhere close by, the ticking of a clock was heard. I thought maybe it was time for me to go and look for my own room and my own bed. I asked what time it was. She didn't know, and the clock didn't know how to speak. It was a long time ago. Maybe it never was. It would be better if it never was. That woman's forearms were covered with thin, tough scars. I felt them with my sense of touch. I knew everything about them. Such scars are made only by the fine blades of SUPER SILVER razors. I was repulsed, but I felt sorry for her, no matter how trite the expression *for her* sounded, I felt sorry for her. And for myself, for that matter. We did not know each other, by mistake we were lying in the same bed, and that was a mistake we could not correct. Down beneath the window, a poplar or linden tree was rustling. I did not understand it. I didn't understand anything. It was dark and I wasn't ashamed to speak because it couldn't be proven that it was me talking. I was talking about something. Perhaps what I am talking about *now*. She wasn't listening to me. We went on further, lying in the dark, not in the dark — in bed, and not further but longer and longer. It could not be said that it was completely dark — it was more like a dense semi-darkness. Ocean waves were lapping on the shore. *There,* where we were lying, we were hundreds of miles from the nearest shore, but the waves were lapping no less on the shore, and that was comforting. That far away murmur of the waves. I touched her swollen eyelids. The dark circles under her eyes. I was almost afraid that she would say: *noli turbare circulos meos.* She said nothing. She did not speak Latin. Neither did I. So I don't know, how could I have been afraid that she would say *noli turbare circulos meos?* I didn't even know what that meant. I was waiting for them to print the morning papers so dawn could break. It didn't seem like dawn would break soon. The night before we had gone to bed early. In our clothes. We lay down because that is how one sleeps. But I couldn't go to sleep no matter what. I counted sheep, I counted forty-eight, there were no more. The rest had been slaughtered. She asked me where I was going to go. As if I had already experienced all of this earlier. It made no sense for me to leave at that moment. She was seriously ill. She had a fever of 106. Doctors were crowding around the room, running into each other in the dark, mumbling, "*morire, moritura, moribunda.*" We did not know what that meant. We did not know Latin. However — what is most interesting — *the village doctor lay beside her, and his horse observed the whole thing through the window.* So, now there were three of us squeezed into a tight bed. I had the impression that I had already read that, somewhere. The doctors had an excellent knowledge of Latin. She must have had a lot of experience with doctors. Under my fingers I felt the thin, tough scars — I detest adjectives — but those scars really were thin and tough, just like those made by the fine blades of SUPER SILVER razors. I felt them with my sense of cutting veins. At this point, the pencil went dull. I don't know how I went on writing. It's not clear to me how I was writing in the darkness at all. Dawn had broken, but at some other longitude. Dawn is always breaking somewhere and somewhere the waves are always murmuring. I didn't ask her any questions, she didn't answer any. I attempted to remember where we had met. I could not. I could not see her face. I doubt that we had ever met. It sometimes happens that I lie down with people I have never met — it is rude — but what can I do about it? I asked her something, she answered something. I think we were holding hands. Our hands were trembling. That, I know. The members of her household were breathing deeply in the next room, while behind another wall someone was coughing constantly. A neighbor. Either he wanted to disturb us or he was dying of tuberculosis. But that was not the reason we were not sleeping. We were not sleeping for no reason. I asked her something, she answered nothing. Then I touched her pussy. Not meaning to scold me, she pushed my hand away and said, "Don't do that. You might get an F on your essay for using that word." Nonsense! As if the teacher could possibly know that I had touched her pussy, as if the teacher had never touched anyone's pussy, and as if I wasn't already going to get an F on this essay even before I started writing it at all. Like in all written assignments, time was passing terribly slowly. I was afraid it might stop. Superstition! It is not clear to me why I wanted so badly for dawn to break. I had nowhere to go. That's an infinitive, isn't it? Didn't she ask me that, and didn't I answer her? I was disgusted by her, but I was holding her hand. I was afraid of the dark and ashamed because she disgusted me. Wasn't she just the same as I am: several elements dissolved in water in a certain ratio, in which *something* flickers and makes it all alive and capable of vanishing and of feeling horrible. And just when I had stopped being disgusted, two guys entered the room, turned on the light, took some things, turned off the light, and went out. She didn't know who they were. I felt like I had met them somewhere. The neighbor kept coughing. I asked her about the origins of the thin, tough scars. She just said, "Death lasts longer than life. It is like a fine membrane between   and   . Something like osmosis." I wanted to ask her about   and   , and she wanted to answer me. I no longer remember what I wanted to ask her, she wanted to answer precisely THAT question, but I didn't ask it. I asked it later. *Just then* she didn't want to answer me. She wanted me to kiss her. I kissed her hand. I did not know how else to kiss. On my lips I felt the thin, tough scars which—for the third time in this essay—are made by the fine blades of SUPER SILVER razors. Or they were made by insomnia. Who knows? On such nights nothing exists except two imaginary people. Again they entered, turned on the light, put some things away, turned off the light, and went out. I was certain I had seen them somewhere. It seemed to me that the night was moving backwards, that dawn would never break, that instead of dawn, dusk would fall again. She wanted me to kiss her. I kissed her cheek. I did not know how else to kiss. In the other room, her father was breathing heavily. Many times he had dreamt that she was lying in bed with an accidental passerby who kissed her on the cheek. He was not breathing heavily because of that. He was breathing heavily because he would die soon. Everyone who breathes soon dies. In the morning, after shaving, he would have to hide the SUPER SILVER razor blades. He had no choice. And the neighbor was constantly coughing. It was more likely that he was dying than just trying to disturb us. I cannot say for sure. I'm just saying: It's more likely! His cough, in any case, was not disturbing us whatsoever. She was learning all of this by heart, like some sort of boring classroom material. She pronounced everything in short sentences, absentmindedly. Like I did. The clock was ticking. No matter how hard I tried, I couldn't manage to read it. In the neighborhood, there were no church towers to recite the hours in a more intelligible way. They weren't there because — as I already said — on nights like those nothing exists except two imaginary people. And even they were no longer there. It all drove me to boredom. *This* essay drove me to boredom: no introduction, development, conclusion, an essay graded automatically — *insufficient, F.* She wanted me to kiss her. I kissed her lips. I did not do otherwise. *I knew* how to kiss. It was as if I wanted to ask her something, as if she wanted to answer me something. I thought about whether to ask her, she thought about whether to answer me. And so on for a long time. We didn't have anything to say. We said that a long time ago. I wanted the essay to be finished as soon as possible. She wanted nothing. I was afraid that I wouldn't make it, that I would leave, that the essay would remain unfinished. I was afraid of the dark. She asked me where I was going to go. Everything was being repeated, and it had been unbearable even the first time. And si-in the-lence, the telephone rang. She did not have a telephone. It rang somewhere in the neighborhood. Perhaps at my place. Maybe the person calling could tell us what was going on. It rang for a long time. Maybe it is still ringing. Fortunately, they had just finished printing the morning newspapers. Dawn should break any minute. As the nights grow longer, the newspapers they print are ever longer. Just then, the neighbor also stopped coughing. Either he died, or he was driven to boredom by it all. She asked me where I was going to go. I had nowhere to go. I got up, went down into the street, bought a paper, and stood there waiting for a tram. Almost ten thousand miles to the east, in Peking, a fine, persistent rain was falling. That only amplified the depressing atmosphere of the morning. The trams were consistently not coming. I headed to school on foot.

My Name is Tmu

my name is tmu, i know it is a stupid name, it is not my fault
whatsoever, they thought me up, others wanted me to be named
tmu, i don't exist, capital letters don't either, i am half from the
imagination of others, half from my own fiction, i do not know if
periods exist, i don't know anything anymore, i am abandoned,
my shoes went somewhere, my overcoat is freezing on a corner
somewhere, my eyes left their sockets and are watching it all
through the window, and all the whores too, like myself a son-of-
a-bitch, like my mother who died before my birth so that i would
have a tough childhood, like everyone else, i am no longer here, i
live in the past, the past can no longer pass, familiar faces are
softened with oblivion, there is no uncertainty, there is no fear,
all of that already happened, nobody says anything, everything
has already been said, somewhere i gasp for breath, of course, my
bronchitis is slowly turning into tuberculosis, i couldn't care in
the least, that is the future, who can know the future, who can
know how much i wanted to put a question mark after *future*, i
will make up for it one day, i will keep my word, now i'm interested in something else—it is not clear to me how i have never
until now tried at least to commit suicide, maybe because i still
think about suicide, in the way that writers do, i pretend *only* to
think about suicide, like a concept, does that mean i am a writer,
i don't think so, i am too lazy for that, someone else is writing
about me, that perfectly fits in with my announcement that i am
imaginary, that is the only thing i know about myself with certainty—the fact that i am imaginary fits in with something,
that's just fine, i won't bear the responsibility, let Him think
about that, I watch him leaning over *this* piece of paper, his dull
pencil torments me, i wonder if he always writes with a pencil,

the son-of-a-bitch, why is he writing at all, perhaps he has a reason, anyway writing is only a little more stupid than living, i said
that i live in the past, that was what *he* wanted, i don't care about
him, i'm bothered by something else—i can't explain the shining
balls in my childhood in any way to myself, long before the writing, they were so inexplicable, useless, intangible, shining so
beautifully, they appeared in the bush—he left out the letter
R—the son-of-a-bitch, a play on words, they appeared, I say,
flickered, hopped about, swarmed together, vanished, passing
through me, if that was me, who can possibly know—so many
people had a difficult childhood—if that was me—the little
balls were an omen of hard times, objects radiating nothingness,
shining out the senselessness of their presence in that place or any
other, in that time or any other, i was awakened by fear of death
or its presence—death is always present—everything was scattered: my shape, my mind, the error that it is *me* suffering, now i
live in that time, thank god that it is only the past, i survived all
that, but ahead of time *he* thought up a SOLITUDE for me, and
then another UNBEARABLE SOLITUDE, and i withstood that
as well, it lasted longer than when it is read, m u c h longer, i
caught my breath, now i can keep my promise, i will insert a
question mark—?—of the two of *us,* who is *I,* i am not, i didn't
believe that capital letters existed, does He exist at all, does writing exist, it must exist since i do, one day i will no longer exist, i
can hardly wait for that fine day, the long-ago-announced death
of literature, yes, people talk about the death of literature and literature is dead, the literary work dies at the moment the writer
finishes the last sentence, it goes on living in the past, everything
sinks further into the past, just like me, like all the whores, i will
go somewhere, but *he* made sure ahead of time that my shoes
would leave, that my overcoat and eyes would leave me, and how
can i go anywhere naked and blind, and barefoot, moreover, perhaps i don't even have legs, no mention of legs was made, *he* is
not such a bad writer, he foresaw everything beforehand, maybe
he's not a bad writer but the conditions he's writing in are unbearable, inhuman, how can i let him know that, better if i don't

even try, He is my maker, for Him there are capital letters, he made me from nothing, he will return me to nothing, when he finishes the last sentence only words will be left of me, all of *this* will be just words, now they are something more, they are *my* life, i lived before this life as well, i was someone, now i am tmu, fortunately it all passed, i am at peace in my past, nothing can surprise me, it is absurd but true, to live one's past again means to free oneself of it, the future isn't coming anyway, it is only a false refrain, in the falling rain, just to make a rhyme, i hear the drizzle of the raindrops on a brass band, an awful, unbearable sound, and this is also ephemeral, when it stops raining here a tin roof will start playing nearby, there is always hope that my shoes, overcoat and eyes will return, my shoes will sooner or later grow tired of futile walking, my overcoat will freeze, my eyes will grow bored with all they are seeing, i will go out then maybe and i will be able to say more about the rain, just to make a rhyme, a banal rhyme, a normal flow of thoughts swollen and murky, it was raining wasn't it, when it rains i like to remember old times, nothing else was left for me, but to rhyme again, i say, i like to remember, to remember the girls i have forgotten, i longed for them, and for all the whores, i let my *soul* go somewhere in the hope that it would join up with their souls in the lands of some sort of comfortable solitude, all just nonsense, a lack of familiarity with the real nature of the soul, that's how i lost myself, wandering off among the monotonous lines without capital letters and punctuation marks, i forgive them, after all i forgive them, long ago they passed away, those girls, they left their past, my eyes saw their death announcements, my ears hear noise at the door, my shoes and overcoat are returning, but not alone, the shoes are on someone's feet, the overcoat on someone's back, is this a visit ??? that's how much i wonder if this is a visit, that would surprise me, i never knew anyone, i thought that *he* and i were alone, endlessly distant like a face and *its* reflection in a mirror, it is a visit after all, the sounds of a visit from the past, who might that be, there is no question mark because i'm not interested in that, it was no one, it is better that way, i will forget everything, i will stop think-

ing, and *he* cannot stop me, i don't know what his name is, the
son-of-a-bitch, he didn't sign his name, he will sign it when he
finishes the last sentence, then it will be too late, i will never learn
who he is, who he is, a tautology, and he is an imaginary character, others gave him a name, he's imagined all kinds of stuff about
himself, just like me, just like all sons-of-bitches, and what can i
change about that, and what is there to be changed anyway, and
where is *that*, and where am i, me, tmu whose grave will be a
page of a magazine, two or three pages in a book, the son-of-a-
bitch, i am sure that he will not be critical enough to burn all of
this, he will let me rot here for years, let all of this repeat, con-
necting the end with the beginning, he's thought something up
for me, he wants others to read about me, i wonder if those others exist, if they exist he wants to tell them something, i don't
know what, he doesn't know what either, they won't know either,
it is not important, at least in my view, i have a feeling that something fateful will happen, it is enough for the commas to disappear and that will be my end, nothing will be left to define me, i
don't know what will happen if the commas vanish, i don't dare
think about it, he does there are no more commas there is nothing was there ever anything vanishing inconceivable the vanishing is not fini is this the end the ultimate end i don't know only
one thing is certain:

Departing

In this life, she *didn't* return several times. There's a chill in my gut which speaks to that. Everything stops for a moment and I know that she was here, just within reach, but then a building complex *accidentally* got between her and me. I don't know her name. I have never seen her, and yet I know all of her typical movements, her gait, her slightly bowed legs. Once upon a time, she was my sister. She existed in those times, in the present which disappeared at the very thought of it. That is why every morning (if I don't hang myself) I look through the newspaper hoping that I will recognize her face in one of the death announcements. I don't know in what way. I'm expecting a phone call from someone who can say more about it all. That is the only way I can be convinced that she lived, but I can never know with certainty if she returned. Did I dream her up? The only thing I'm sure of is that she departed, departed for a terribly long time, enjoyed departing, departed twice, three times at once, she rejected everything that might be interpreted to be a coincidence and—I must admit—I never met anyone who departed so skillfully, departed so long, even longer than this sentence, and then she departed just a bit more, I think, so that she could depart before she even arrived; she departed until she remained only on the horizon, and after that even less, so that then the hungry dogs could come by, eat that as well, and die in the worst of pain. And it wasn't just that she departed—she went on departing in the past tenses; first she departed in the simple past, then in the perfect, and then she departed and departed all the way up to the past perfect and there it was no longer known whether she ever returned or not, because the past perfect is such a tense that the difference between what *is* and what *was not* is negligible. Perhaps she did not exist, but just returned; perhaps she existed, but did not return. And if she did not return—she did not return with remarkable punctuality—on Wednesdays at 4:30. On Wednesdays I was always somewhere else. Never in the same place. I might recognize her. I read that somewhere, or someone wrote something like that, so she would return or not return, or all of that at once, or none of that at all. She *didn't* return on foot, but she departed on the tram. If she did return, then she was always doing something, she emptied spittoons full of sputum that looked like embryos, she wiped away the stench, some kind of stench—I don't remember what kind—she said *I will always return* and huffed because she was working hard. Why did she return? Because she was using me? pity? or *because*. I don't know. I'm expecting a phone call from someone who can say more about it all. *Perhaps because.* That is quite enough reason for someone to return, and more than enough reason for departure. There was nothing I could change about that. I had no face, I had no body. I didn't wish to change anything. *That place* where I stayed was nothing but a foggy supposition. I didn't uncover all the *circumstances*. I was not even interested in them. Something like a thread! What might it have been? A countless number of exclamation marks, a countless number of question marks. There was nothing. I always thought that *always* would last longer. Did she return or not? It makes no difference! Once someone leaves, then it really makes no difference whether they return or not. I hope it is true, although it is not and so I hope that it is not, so that the possibility exists that it is. A countless number of question marks? A countless number of exclamation marks!

Maxims

I woke up at exactly 7:30. I lay there a while longer, in fact I
tried to go back to sleep, but I had no luck. The night before
I had gone to sleep around 10:30. Eight hours of sleep is quite
enough. I read that in a magazine. I think that was yesterday. No!
It was the day before yesterday. Since I remembered that, I gave
up on any further attempt to go back to sleep. I got up, looked
for my house shoes, put them on and went into the bathroom. I
turned on the water, not too hot, not too cold—the way I like
it most—and by the way, out of habit, I looked at myself in the
mirror. I didn't see anything. My face wasn't there. I am not a
man who panics easily. I raised my hand to touch my face and instead of my face I touched—if *touch* is the right way to say it—
emptiness. Then I saw that, in fact, my hand wasn't there, that I
had only thought it would be good to touch my face and assure
myself it was there. I don't know how I saw that: If there is no
face, there are no eyes either. And yet, I saw it. My house shoes
were under the sink—that means I was there—and the water
was running from the faucet; it was draining away in vain, and
I could do nothing to stop the waste. "What a horrible dream,"
I thought and decided to wake up. Dreams are just dreams! But
alas, I was not in bed. I could clearly see the empty bed, the
twisted sheets, and my pajamas tossed on top of them. That was
too much even for a man with nerves of steel like myself. I had
to find help. I had no choice. That meant I would have to knock
on my neighbor's door—people are here to help one another—
but that gave rise to another problem: how to show up in front
of my neighbor with nothing, I mean without even myself. Maybe I should have gone anyway—necessity is the mother of inven-
tion—but my will could not put anything in motion. I mean my

feet. They weren't there. Still, I was not discouraged. Even in the most difficult circumstances one must keep one's wits about oneself. The day had started poorly, no argument there, but it would have been worse—God forbid—if I hadn't woken up at all and never learned anything more about myself. My horoscope had predicted a difficult week. Full of ups and downs. That's a good saying. I always believed you should live according to wise sayings. At the moment, things were going badly, but sooner or later things would start going better. I'm convinced of it. I am an optimist. Even if this state of things lasts for a while, the old saying brings me comfort: Nobody is irreplaceable. Such is life! Until a while ago I was lounging about in my comfortable bed, trademark SIMPO SAN, and now all that was left of me was ... In fact, I don't know what was left of me. And yet, something was. Better something than nothing. But all of that is still irrevocably vanishing. Not me! I am still here somewhere in some way. My surroundings! Reflecting on this and that, I had paid no attention to my surroundings—that was my fatal error—and then the bathroom and the bedroom and everything vanished. Only my self remained, in some sort of grey emptiness. I will have to be more careful, I will have to take better care of my self and try to get out of here. I have to learn as much as possible about the rules of the game that are in place here. Because, you live and learn.

Fin Who is Sitting

I am sitting, leaning against the wall, and my name is Fin. That's all I'm doing. I can do nothing more for myself. I have done all I could. I was asleep, and then I woke up, I wanted to rub my eyes with my hands, but my hands were not there. I had to wake up again. My face was covered with my palms, I was sitting with my back to the wall, my name was Fin. I wasn't sure if my name was really Fin, or if I had shortened some longer name so that I could be named as little as possible. I knew that I was on the wrong side of the wall. When they finally decide to tear it down, the wall will collapse on me. I know this from experience: they always collapse on me. Even if by some miracle I was able to move to the other side, nothing would change. The wall would collapse on that side. Such is my fate, but the walls weren't wrong, the sides of the walls weren't wrong—I was wrong. I was conceived from a splitting, once long ago, I don't know when, they didn't tell me. They told me something else, some kind of lie full of adjectives, something fittingly filthy. *Something* preceded those events, something shapeless split him and me. His name was Tmu. He died soon after. We never met. That is not important. What is important is that I am speaking into the wind. The wall is near a beach, the waves are murmuring, there's plenty of wind, and raincoats walk holding hands on the edge of the horizon. I find it unimaginable that anyone dares to exist without covering their face with their hands. I always hold my face in my hands. I observe my surroundings through the cracks between my fingers. As time has passed, that narrow vision has become wider, my fingers have grown thin because of erosion, but if I were to uncover my face completely I would die of shame. I did nothing wrong, I didn't do anything, I hurt no one, but I would die of shame simply be-

cause I am still *something*. I'm just sitting, and shame is tearing
me apart. I'm wasting away from shame. Soon, my name will be
Fi, and then F, and then I will just be *named*, I will be anyone, no
one will be able to blame me for anything. The shame will still go
on breathing along with me until the wind finally turns me into
dust. As long as I am—I will breathe for two. More for the
shame than for myself. Nothing I can do about that. I am sitting,
leaning against the wall, and my name is Fin. That has a rhythm
to it, it fits in perfectly. I was not created in the splitting—they
just lied to me to be merciful—I gave birth to myself, my own
responsibility, out of nothing; I was born really old, I knew nothing about myself, I didn't believe in myself. Why would I believe
in myself if I am already *nothing*? It is enough that I am sitting
and that my name is Fin. I have company here with me: A spider
and a dog. The spider is named Fin. And the dog is named Fin. I
can hardly see them sometimes through the spaces between my
fingers. Fin has spun a web between my ear and the wall. His web
is worn out, maybe he moved into an abandoned spider web,
poor Fin, all day long he is unmoving, maybe he is dead, with
spiders you can never tell, flies don't get caught in his web, it is
impossible to catch anything in that web, because the web has
been spun between me, and I am impossible, and it's the wall
which is wrong. The dog has been dead for ages. All day long he
is de com pos ing in to syl la bles right here next to me. He doesn't
do anything else. That is enough. At least he rhymes. At the same
time, he really stinks. He stinks so badly that it overwhelms my
stench. I don't blame him. Aren't we all named Fin, aren't we all
more or less dead, are we not sitting, leaning against the wall,
helpless to do anything for ourselves or for others? And anyway, if
I've already been thrown into the garbage heap as useless, what
else can I expect except stench? But I don't even expect that. I am
sitting, leaning against the wall. When I get tired I go to sleep.
When I'm asleep, my name is not Fin and I am not sitting, leaning against the wall. In my sleep I dream, my name is something
else—afterwards I always forget that name—and I constantly
dream the same dream, but it is not the dream of *that* particular

sleep, it is a memory of a dream that I dreamt as a child. When awake, no matter how hard I try to remember the past, no matter how hard I struggle against oblivion just to learn how I used to be, I always see myself sitting, leaning against the wall, and my name is Fin. It must be that I have been on the garbage heap longer than I remember. In that dream I am walking down the street that leads to my teacher's house. All along the way, I am lured by prostitutes hidden behind the trunks of chestnut trees. I hesitate, struggle to resist them, and finally I reach my teacher's downstairs window. The window is open. I can see my teacher in the light of hundreds of candles correcting our homework, an essay on the topic of INSOMNIA. Leaning way into the room, suspecting some sort of injustice, I cry out so loudly that the candle flames flicker, "Teacher!" She turns to me, our faces are so close to each other that I feel her breath coming from her nose, but instead of my teacher's gentle eyes there are two lifeless panes of glass through which I can see myself: I am sitting, leaning against the wall, and my name is Fin. That's all I'm doing. I can do nothing more for myself, for the hundredth, thousandth time—I can do nothing more for myself. I was asleep, and then I woke up. Perhaps I was talking in my sleep. I didn't hear anything. Did anyone hear anything? Perhaps they did. Through the spaces between my fingers, from my prison, I can see some sort of radial crack, some sort of blotch on the wall across from me. The longer I look, the smaller the crack becomes. From that senseless blotch of vertical and horizontal lines, the contours of a man emerge, with wide shoulders, a hook nose and low forehead. There's no doubt: it all fits in with the appearance of a human being. Suddenly, this being turns angrily and says to me, "Fin, you son-of-a-bitch, I heard everything. You went to see teach to ask for a passing grade." And then he goes on observing me like an enemy with his little eyes deeply planted in their sockets. He is only a foot high, and he is only an accidental shape of some sort of crack, but he looks at me arrogantly, as if he knows what he wants, so I cast my eyes downward, blush, and watch Fin who is de com pos ing while millions of maggots who are also called Fin are crawling all over him. The language with which I'm saying this doesn't exist. I know that is impossible, but it is stronger than me. This need to speak into the wind, to speak although I have nothing to say, to say that *nothing*. This is just one small nothingness hardly enough to cause a minor neurosis in a feeble little girl, but it needs to be said, and in order to be said I have to be sitting and to be named Fin, to speak about that in a dead language, no matter how impossible that is, to constantly be wondering how all of that is possible, how it is at all possible that I compose such a long sentence about something so insignificant, not being able moreover to put a question mark at the end, because even question marks are impossible! That I can sit, be named Fin and speak—someone else takes care of that. He comes by every month. He must live very far away. He brings food, not out of pity but because there are some people who think logically —such people surely exist—who wonder how it is possible to sit and be named Fin without food and water. It is not possible. He knows that very well and I know that very well. I do not need food. How can I eat when my face is covered with my hands? He does care about that. He brings food so that the story can be logical. He doesn't care whether I eat or not. And that's all. For the umpteenth time I am sitting, leaning against the wall, and my name is Fin. That is how I feel most comfortable. I don't know anything about myself. I just talk to myself and I will keep talking until the wind and rain make me formless once again. *Something* formless. From me, two will quickly come about, through splitting. One will die. He will not know me. I will hate them inside them, inside them I will not believe in them. I finally learned my lesson. Otherwise I would not be able to talk about it. About the past. The past is incomprehensible to me. I am in the present, and the present lasts too briefly for anything to happen inside it, except for itself. I do not happen at all. I only imagine. Here, somewhere on the beach, the night sky is scattered with stars. There has been no night for ages. That is because I no longer rotate with the earth. I grew bored with that monotonous rotating. I would rather be sitting, leaning against the wall, and I would rather my name be Fin. The waves are splashing on me, crushing me against the cliffs, on me it says FLY TWA. I don't know what that means. I don't know if it really means FLY TWA, or if I shortened some longer meaning so that it could mean as little as possible. I dn't knw wht tht mns. That's what happens. Suddenly, the vowels vanished. Then I sleep. I sleep among the silkworms, I don't bother them, I only sleep when they are also asleep. I get up before them so that they won't wake to find me among them. I am sitting, leaning against the wall, and my name is Fin. That's all I'm doing. Fin is de com pos ing, the spi der web is teaaaaring, the sto ry is dis in te grat ing, everything dis solves in to the night.

A Sentence Torn From Context

... in the darkness, groping around and bumping into things, I looked for the bed which was not in its usual place but in quite a different one, and the possibility existed that there was no bed in that room at all, so, tormented by the length of the sentence, I decided to sleep leaning against the wall, hoping that sleep could distinguish between *up, down, left, right,* but sleep differentiated them quite well, and anyway there weren't any walls, that's not what this was about, so I thought: maybe there is no bed in this room, maybe I went into the wrong room, and I went out into the hall where there was a series of identical doors on both sides, and I was no longer *in any room at all,* and that lessened the chances that I would finally go to sleep and made the situation even more difficult—it is difficult to go to sleep if you do not know where you are—but I didn't give up, there was still hope that I would find myself although it was late and it was a little unpleasant to enter the other rooms, in the darkness, groping around and bumping into things, to look for the room that I was *really* in—I rejected the possibility that I was not to be found in any of the rooms without giving it further reflection—and then the notion occurred to me that I had fallen asleep long ago and that I was only dreaming that I was looking for the room I was in along an endless hallway, so I thought: excellent, I will stand *here* and wait until I wake up, but I could not define that *here* in a space of endless and identical doors and it took a lot of time for me to comprehend the hopelessness of my position, to realize that the hallway had neither beginning nor end, that I was just an undefined character in a fragment of a sentence whose meaning I could not determine, a sentence torn from the context of a portentous story that I knew nothing about ...

Letter to Skopje

It's been an eternity since I got a letter from you. Maybe it's my turn to write. I've been working a lot these days, so I thought it was your turn. I joked with your green eyes in a park. The kids there pointed at me, laughed and said, "He's crazy!" Am I crazy because I am writing you letters while drinking countless bottles of beer? In the morning, I have a headache. And I have bronchitis. It's hard for me to breathe. I am afraid that you don't love me anymore because I don't write. Moreover, there is no elevator in my building. The president of our building collective is Chinese, his body has slanted surfaces and he worries because the postmen are coming around ever more rarely. I understand him completely. You know, it is quite dangerous. Buildings where the postmen stop coming soon stop existing. That is the way the world order works. After that, letters make no sense any more. I am becoming more and more afraid. The neighbors always fall asleep before the end of the television broadcast, they don't turn off their TV set, so there is nothingness all night long on their screens. The hissing can be heard quite well: SSSHHHHHHH! And how can one sleep then? And I am so afraid to write. Stories should be written like letters are written: quickly, illiterately, illegibly; then you should just put them into orange envelopes and send them to hell! But other people write my letters. They are anonymous letters. However, when I overcome my laziness and get down to writing, then my letters arrive on Monday. Tuesday at the latest. Isn't that so? Not to mention what happened the other evening: You won't believe it. The evening before last I was going down a street (as a pedestrian), and quite by accident I peeked in through the smudged glass of a shop window, and at the counter I saw a sad watchmaker, hunched over with a magnifying glass on one eye, fixing a tick-tocking little machine for measuring time, which does not exist at all. And how could I have been angry because you did not show up that evening? That evening did not exist, just as this one does not, just as evenings don't exist at all. Those are just dark words. Just so that we could have something to talk about in the evening. I felt sorry for the watchmaker. I don't know how it is where you are, but in Titovo Užice, the saddest people are the watchmakers. It is no wonder. That is why I fed his pigeons. That was all I could do for him. But! Listen, if one evening—and this, of course will never happen—if the evening really does exist, and I show up at your place and ring your bell—will you open your umbrella for me? You don't have to answer that question! You don't have to answer the next one either because I'm not going to ask it. I'm warning you ahead of time: I am going to publish everything! Everyone who reads these lines will die sooner or later. Nothing about that can be changed. But I will still feel guilty because I will feel responsible for their death. Now, what's done is done! All of them will be born once again. One as an oak, another as a polar bear, another as the letter O! Depending on the possibilities. But it's already very late. I wonder if you will understand me! Yes! All night long, if I had enough space, I would repeat will you understand me, will you understand me, will you understand me . . .

Providence

It rained hard all afternoon. A woman in her thirties came into the bookstore, tapped the tip of her umbrella on the floor to shake off the raindrops, and began to look through the books. The impression was that she intended to buy nothing and that she had entered the bookstore just to get out of the rain. This didn't go unnoticed by the salesman and so he didn't bother her. But the woman unexpectedly approached him and asked, "Do you have Svetislav Basara's *Vanishing Tales*?"

"*Vanishing Tales . . . Vanishing Tales*," mumbled the salesman as if trying to remember, and then coming back from his reflections, he said politely, "Unfortunately, we don't. They have all vanished."

The Perfect Crime*

* First Appeared as "Savrsen zlocin" in *Peking by Night*, 1985

Once everything is over, what is the sense of chronology? So, I will start just anywhere: Gruber had three brothers. Not one of them is significant to the story. Gruber himself is hardly of significance to the story. The day when the unknown girl was killed, Gruber ran into a gentleman at the door of the main post office. After that, he went for a beer. Before doing so, he apologized because he was not an impolite person. The postal worker at window five glanced at the clock at that very moment: it was 8:10. Ten minutes later I looked at my watch: it was 8:10. I was across the street from the main post office, but I did not see the incident at the door; I was gaping at the cover-page of a foreign magazine in the window of the newsstand. On the cover there was a woman naked to the waist, and under the picture it said, in bold letters: **HAPPY NEW YEAR 1963**. That only proves that lechery is a vice because, if I had been looking toward the post office, I would have seen that it was 8:10. Thus, one thing has been established, we have a single fact, but it is not significant to the story. Facts are never of any significance to the story.

Actually, we never know what is happening; we are only straws in the winds of events, the facts come at the end. The same is also true of stories: "The theory of relativity can be applied in totality to the world of the novel; in real prose, in no way less than in Einstein's world, there is no place for the omniscient narrator."* At that moment, a moment before or a moment after, the girl who was to be killed asked me what time it was. I said it was 8:10, asking myself: what sense is there in factualism when things are already happening? My watch must have stopped, because when I went into the post office to mail a letter, I saw by the clock on the wall that it was 8:35. The postal worker at window five asked:

* J.P. Sartre

"Normal mail, registered, or express?" He had one foot in the grave. As did I, as do we all, for it says clearly in the Vulgate "*Nescimus horam neque diem.*"* I said "express" because that was the last thing I had heard. I repeated it like an echo. But at least I had one fact. My watch had stopped. That fact had a certain significance to the story, because it brought about the following train of thought: "I wound it last night. Why did it stop? It must be broken. It hasn't even been three months since I bought it." Then I remembered that Doc Holiday in a certain novel said, "I have known people who wear the watches they inherited from their fathers, who inherited them from their fathers in turn . . ." and I gave a bitter laugh, lamenting the good old days when things were solidly made and durable. Thereby, we have come to another fact: in the old days things were solid and durable. That is a sort of lie, like most facts, because if it really were that way, there would be no need for the appearance of new, unsolid and undurable things in the world.

Coming out of the post office I went to the bar were Gruber had also gone to drink a beer after running into that particular gentleman. In doing so, I made a concession to chronology, because Gruber was no longer in the bar. Of course, I had no way of knowing that; I did not even know that he had gone to the bar. How could I know since "in real prose, in no way less than in Einstein's world, there is no place for the omniscient narrator?" Apart from that, he had had enough time to drink his beer and leave. As for me, I did not go to the bar to have a cup of watery coffee, but rather to open up my watch and, perhaps, discover why it had broken. With my pocket knife, I took off the back, which was inscribed with the words "Antimagnetic, Waterproof"; everything was—at least it seemed to the layman—all right in the mechanism: there were no broken springs, bent cogs, no disorder whatsoever. For a while I looked at the little pieces of metal which had been constructed to ensure the flow of time—now useless. Attempting to close the back of the watch, I did something wrong. One of the springs leapt from its place and—sailing

* "We know neither the hour nor the day." (Trans.)

some four or five yards—struck the neck of a lady who was sitting by the window. As a consequence, I looked in that direction and saw a girl that I knew from somewhere; it was the girl
who had asked me what time it was and had gotten the wrong
information (which was not my fault but the fault of the broken spring), and who would be killed later that day. But not yet
at that time. Simultaneously, I heard the voice of the lady at the
table by the window. Looking at the girl, she was telling her lady
friend something, of which I only understood, ". . . I think he'll
never forgive her for that. He's not the type to forgive something
like that. I'm telling you, dear, Karlo is a dangerous man." Gruber
was still in the bar, which is evidence that the omniscient narrator really does not exist. However, I could not have known that.
Several people were drinking their mugs of beer (I wondered how
they could drink such terrible stuff); I did not know Gruber. I
only knew that he liked beer. I will never meet Gruber. "So, when
I leave the bar," I thought, "I will throw this broken watch away."

   That afternoon, I have no idea what time it might have
been—my watch was (this is another in the trail of facts) broken and had been thrown away—I met a friend and we went
for a drink at a café. On the window of the café it said "caffe,"
which bothered my friend because he was a French teacher. "That
doesn't mean anything," he explained, "*Café* is properly written
with one *f* and an *é* at the end, so it should be *café*." At that instant it began to bother me as well. It had not bothered me earlier
because I had not known the rules of French orthography. Besides, the owner of the café had a glass eye, or maybe both his
eyes were glass, which would bring about the visual effect. I was
also angry at myself: if I had not been gaping at naked women
in the windows of newsstands I would have known what time it
was. But, that is a fact, already proven, and it is useless to fight
against the facts. The facts lead us to our death, that is also incontrovertible, and I think there is no reason to explain why. While
I was surrendering to these reflections, my friend had already
asked me several questions which I, perhaps not in the correct
order, memorized: how are you? what are you doing? why didn't

you call last week as we agreed? are you still writing in the first person? are you finally going to start writing a novel? I started answering, perhaps in reverse order: I'm fine, and you? I forgot to call; nothing special, I'm writing a short story on the perfect crime, of course — in the first person, but that doesn't mean anything because, as Michel Butor wrote:

> The narrator is not purely the first person. He is never completely the writer himself. One should never confuse Robinson Crusoe and Daniel Defoe, or Marcel and Proust. The narrator himself is imaginary, but in that world of fictional characters, he is the writer's representative. Let us not forget that he is also the reader's representative, or more precisely, he is that standpoint which the writer leads the reader to in order to get him to evaluate and follow the sequence of events so that he can use them.

It seems I will never start my novel. Then I said, "Look at that girl across the street. This is the third time I've seen her today. That's weird. This morning she asked me what time it was." "What's weird?" my friend asked. "You run into some people every day and you don't think that's weird at all."

This was also a fact. Quite a few facts had begun to pile up: 1. Lechery is a vice; 2. my watch stopped; 3. in the good old days things were solid and durable; 4. the watch was broken and thrown away; 5. if I had not been looking at the picture of the naked woman, I would have known what time it was; 6. facts lead us to our deaths; 7. I run into some people everyday and do not see anything strange in that. I thought about these facts, I tried to find some kind of hidden connection between them, with no success whatsoever, I must admit. I had even overlooked one fact: before I met my friend, I do not know how long before, I saw two men standing there, in the street by the market, I do not know the street's name, and they caused a certain disharmony in the process of perception, because one usually does not run into two such men together. Namely, one was elegant, overly

elegant and heavily perfumed, which I established a few seconds
later when I passed by them and heard the other one, wearing a
leather jacket and jeans, saying, "It's a deal, Karlo." Not far from
there, perhaps as decor, there was a yellow truck, RABA by make,
standing in sharp contrast to the warm green of the market, but
perhaps it was just a prop placed by Providence, calculated to
make me notice the truck, because I am not really a truck lover.
Several streets further down, Gruber passed by the girl. This
should be understood as a bad sign because a week before that
Gruber had been at the hospital, briefly, to pick up a health certi-
ficate. That day three people died in the internal medicine ward.
This should be kept in mind.

The other indicative fact (again a fact) was that, after the for-
malities, I talked with my friend about death. First, my friend
told the owner of the café about the incorrect orthography of
caffe. "I know that," the owner justified himself. "But if I write
caffe with just one *f* then it does not look aristocratic enough, and
people will think my bar is just a plain old beer joint." He had
only one glass eye. I did not fail to notice.

"You see," said my friend, as I was not failing to notice that
the owner of the café had only one glass eye, "when a man dies,
his past no longer makes any sense. With the disappearance of
the subject, everything which connected him to space and time
also disappears; after doing their job, events become absolutely
nothing: *ouk on*.* Thus, it is a great mistake to call someone's biography a *description of life*; biographies are actually *descriptions of
death*, as Albahari would say. And that's why I can't understand
why so much significance is given to the past, to memories, to
facts. It is all just a mask on the face of death. Those who say they
love life, love death in disguise. And that is also why only rare
individuals attain the knowledge that man is an immortal being."

"I agree," I said. "Death is really crafty, although, in the final analysis, it does not exist. But even so, since death has killed
countless people, it has more experience in such things than any
individual, because we can only die once. Nothing can be done

* "Non-existent" (Trans.)

about it. That's a fact. The most we can hope to learn is that we can't know anything for sure, that things and events escape our conceptual abilities and logic, and that there is no place for the omniscient narrator."

Then, Gruber entered the café. Of course, I had no way of knowing that because I am not an omniscient narrator. If I had known, I would have taken it as a bad sign. Purely out of superstition, because Gruber is not a bad guy. Didn't he politely apologize to that gentleman he ran into, even though it was the gentleman's fault? Gruber stood at the bar and ordered a beer. That Gruber fellow really likes beer. Someone in the bathroom flushed the toilet. But no one came out.

"Listen," I said to my friend, as I pointed at the bar, "that man is named Gruber."

It was already getting dark outside. I justified this by the fact (again) that it was late autumn and that the days were getting shorter and shorter. But a day can never be this short. My friend left to go teach his afternoon classes at the high school. Then he said, "See you later." Or vice versa.

I went for a walk. Randomly, carrying a MAP OF THE TOWN in my hand. With a marker, I made dots on the map locating all the important places I passed. There was a large number of black dots.

I wondered if I was giving too much significance to Gruber? Was he not, perhaps, like those characters in Agatha Christie's novels who are the most suspicious, and who only conceal the real criminal? Apart from that, Gruber was arrested that evening because he was drunk and made a scene in the café. But that is not important to the story. It is important that, just in front of the door of my building, I saw the girl again: she was approaching me on the sidewalk, so I stopped. Should I wait for her? Observe her more closely? Should I ask her, "Does the name Karlo mean anything to you?" But the girl suddenly stepped out into the street. I turned away, resolved to wash my hands of the whole affair. I pushed the door handle and thus made a semantic error because it said PUSH on the door, and then there was the sound of squealing brakes, then a dull thud, like the thud of the billy-club hitting someone at the police station nearby where they were beating Gruber. The girl was lying beneath the wheels of a yellow truck, RABA by make, and she looked like my sister's doll which I had once broken . . . but that was a long time ago. I noticed that on the sidewalls of the tires, in worn out letters it said PIRELLI . . .

Once again, I laid out the facts chronologically: 1. Lechery is a vice; 2. my watch stopped; 3. in the good old days things were solid and durable; 4. the watch was broken and thrown away; 5. if I had not been looking at the picture of the naked woman, I would have known what time it was; 6. facts lead us to our deaths; 7. I run into some people everyday and don't see anything strange in that; 8. I heard a man in a leather jacket telling his elegant companion "It's a deal, Karlo."; 9. in the café, I talked about death with my friend; 10. death has a lot more experience with death than anyone else. That was all. I did not manage to find any kind of logical connection between the enumerated facts.

"Agatha Christie is wrong," I thought as I climbed the stairs. "The perfect crime exists after all. But it would not be perfect if someone learned of it. Thus, it is enough just to disturb chronology and factualism a little bit, to twist the logic, and then the whole business can be put down as an ACCIDENT . . ."

Entering my room, I sat at my desk and connected all the dots I had made on the map during my walk. Before my very eyes appeared the contours of a fish—the central symbol in the metaphysical heraldry of the city. Then I remembered that I had not known all day what time it was. I looked at the clock. I sighed. It was 8:10.

Civil War Within

1

Here is a brief account of several mysterious deaths that occurred at the home of my friend, Valdemar Sandoz. That day, not suspecting anything, Sandoz and I were sitting there, being quiet. I knew that Sandoz's house was built in the wrong place, but later on they did not allow this to be a mitigating circumstance for me. All houses are built in the wrong places. It was enough that the first human residence be built in the wrong place and the *circulus vitiosus* was thereafter unbreakable. The mysterious effects of subterranean waters and telluric radiation have brought the species of Homo Sapiens to the point that its members are becoming highly intelligent earthworms. Just as Aristotle says: "A small error at the beginning leads to big errors in the end." Perhaps I am exaggerating; earthworms cannot make coffee. Anyhow, Sandoz made coffee. Then he asked me:

"Do you know what I dreamed about last night?"

"Yes," I said.

"How could you know?"

"Simply enough. We all dream the same dreams. There are no great dreams any more, only a few are left. Even then, it's like stacking the cards in poker. Once you understand the system, you always know who has what in their hands. Or what they are dreaming. Your dream—nothing special. Two pairs, sevens and tens . . . One of those hands you can bet a single chip on, two at the most. You're not one of those who wins at dreams."

"Exactly," said Sandoz, not without a bit of melancholy. "But why are there no women here? At least those lifeless mannequins from the shop windows of the clothing stores that we used to look at back in 1963, '64, '65 . . . Do you remember the mannequins?"

I tried, but could not. A black hole. Infinite darkness in which eternal rain is falling. And besides, all of those stores have long since closed. Everything in them has been sold, everything spent, torn up, squandered. What good does it do to remember things that do not exist any more?

"No, Sandoz," I said. "I cannot remember. But I will tell you what I dreamed about."

"Didn't you just say that we all dream the same dreams?"

"Yes, but this one is just a bit different. I dreamed that I was writing a novel. Of course, that is a normal dream. But then a character named Hans got involved. I mean, someone else was dreaming that he was writing a novel at the same time, and so I found myself together with Hans in a street somewhere. Somewhere in Morocco. Or in Tunis. Since the writer didn't know what to do with me, I started thinking to myself. And suddenly I realized I was alone. I went slowly back up the street because, otherwise, I wouldn't know where to go. The whole street was full of watchmakers' shops. Even though I was in a hurry, and even though I was scared, I peered into the shop windows, driven by a collector's passion for clocks. There were many kinds of clocks, indescribably beautiful, so beautiful that they could never be found in the outside world, in the waking world whose time does not deserve such instruments for measurement in the first place. One of them especially caught my attention, for its hands were moving erratically, and it had two little numeric counters at the corners: one of the second hands was turning in the conventional way, right to left, and the other, to my great astonishment, in the opposite direction. "The perfect chronometer," I thought, "a mechanism which keeps up with all the bifurcations of time." At that very instant I spied Hans. He was coming out of a side street, dressed in some kind of a toga, something like a priest's robes. "Hans," I called. "Take me back to the place in the novel where we parted." Hans placed his finger to his lips, and out of his skirts he pulled an amulet which he shoved into my hands. Then I woke up. The amulet looked like this:

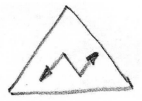

Sandoz carefully regarded the sketch of the amulet which I drew on the back of his daughter's eighth grade report card. He shook his head suspiciously. No doubt he thought it was some kind of black magic symbol. Sandoz was obsessed with black magic. In his final year of architectural studies, instead of designing some kind of factory, workers' hall, or house, he wrote a dissertation about the pentagram (colloquially: the five-pointed star) on our national banner ... the multitude of pentagrams on buildings, mountain tops, soldiers' caps, how all of them had conjured up a pack of demons who had devastated everything, sent a good part of the population straight to hell, for a pittance of a salary of around one hundred dollars a month, at that. In order to bring him back from his dark thoughts, I decided to have a drink. I opted for a "Valentino" cocktail. Into a rather large glass I poured 0.5 cl of vodka, 0.5 cl of Cuban rum, 1 cl of red wine, 0.6 cl of creme-de-menthe, 15 cl of beer, and 1 cl of cold chamomile tea; I stirred it all thoroughly, put in several ice cubes and then drank it.

Sandoz was observing me like I was Fidel Castro.

"Go ahead," I said, "just go on. Ask me the question."

"What question are you talking about?"

"The question you have been wanting to ask me for years. How can I drink such idiotic cocktails?"

"Indeed, how can you drink that swill?"

"There is an answer to every question, as long as the question is of no significance, or if it is idiotic. Real questions have no answers. You see, I drink two or three, indeed even four tall glasses of such an ambrosia, I sit outside in the summer garden of the "Town Café," open up the *Financial Times*, poke a hole in the paper and watch the girls who are hanging around. Nothing nicer than women. But only from a distance. For, when you watch through a hole in a newspaper, you feel like God. You see everything, no one sees you. After all, that is theologically justified: by distancing yourself from the world, you draw near to God. But, that is painful. Because, when you draw even just a bit closer to God, you finally understand what a swine you are, and what a worthless person you are . . ."

"Listen," Sandoz said, "you've fallen under the influence of Martin Luther. You're looking at things too darkly."

"You mean the black preacher the racists killed in America?"

Sandoz frowned. Then he smiled. Finally he began to cry.

"No, no, and again no. That was Martin Luther King. I mean the Luther who threw his inkwell at the devil."

I did not want to get into a theological debate. So, I made myself another cocktail. I offered one to Sandoz as well. Even though I knew he never drinks. This upset him even more (which will later prove to be disastrous), and he shouted:

"You know very well that I don't drink!"

I knew it very well. But, what could I do? Sandoz is really my best friend. I really do love him, insofar as I am able to love, but often I still get on his nerves, and he on mine. After all, whether they love or hate each other—people have to destroy each other.

"True. But how could the future readers of our biographies know that? How will they be able to differentiate the hero, the anti-alcoholic, from the bad guy with a weakness for alcohol?"

"Quit playing around," said Sandoz sullenly, "I'm not Roland Barthes. I don't have an ear for postmodernism. You're losing your sense for the little things that make life better."

"Can anything make life better?" I asked.

And I crossed myself.

2

Sandoz broke the clock and started the tape recorder.

"One, two . . . One, two . . . testing."

He rewound the tape, checked to see if everything was all right, cleared his throat and began to narrate.

"I had a colleague at the university who read too much Plato. What's wrong with that, one might ask. Nothing, of course, but this guy began to overdo it. He took every word literally. You know the myth in *The Symposium* which says that people, before the gods split them in half, were round and that they used to roll around like balls. Well, this friend of mine decided to become whole again, to quit depending on fate, women, local cooperatives, the weather outside, and he started to eat like crazy. He wanted to get so fat that he would be a perfect sphere. Pure idealism. He ate, and ate, and ate. He neglected all his responsibilities just so he could eat more food. Even that wouldn't have been so bad, had he not gotten involved in some rather fishy business: dealing heroin and gunrunning for Arab terrorist groups. He needed a lot of money. I've already said: he ate like crazy. He became the fattest at the university, then in the city, then in the republic, and finally in all of Yugoslavia. Once, for the celebration of Tito's birthday on May 25th, they presented him, as a curiosity, to comrade Tito. Tito said "Comrades, under communism we will all look like this." These words were tumultuously applauded by the Young Pioneers, non-commissioned officers, secret police, and high government officials. Quite a success. But not the only one. There were also several stories about him in *Start*, *TV Guide*, and *Arena*. However, everyone looked at him askance. The rabble does not like it when someone rises above the average, even as an idiot. Today, even idiots must be mediocre. Anyway, so much for the famous motto: *liberté, fraternité, égalité.* And my friend ended up as a sumo wrestler in Kyoto. No, in Osaka. It must be Osaka. Now, why do you watch girls through a hole in the *Financial Times?*"

Sandoz turned off the tape recorder and began to reassemble the fragments of the clock.

Stupid question, I thought. The *Financial Times* is a serious newspaper. Should I do my spying through *Sports* or the *Evening News*? But once I got into some really bad trouble because of the *Financial Times.* A whole bunch of bad trouble.

Suddenly, three photojournalists burst into the room. Their flashes went off two or three times, and they receded into the darkness.

"This is too much!" cried Sandoz. "Modern countries are nothing more than common crap. There is no longer any kind of privacy. No laws. Why, just the other evening, this lieutenant bursts into my house with a couple dozen soldiers. He tells me they'd gotten lost on their way home from the war. They slept here, in my living room. They wanted to set up their tents! To start a campfire. I barely managed to convince them not to do it. Finally, they left just before dawn. And my stupid daughter went with them. She fell in love overnight with the lieutenant. So, now I use her report card to keep score when we play spades. But to be quite honest, they did leave a signed notice behind, a piece of paper which says: *This is to confirm that the third platoon slept here.* Stamp. Signature."

"Yes," I said, "notices, papers. I had an incomparably worse experience with them. After the war, after one of the wars, the devil knows which one, they arrested my father. I don't know why. I was too young to remember. Soon after, a blue envelope arrived, and in the envelope there was a notice: *This is to confirm that we have shot your father as an enemy of the people.*"

"Yes," Sandoz replied, "the mania is spreading. More and more often I catch myself after lunch wanting to write on a piece of paper: *This is to confirm that the turkey on sauerkraut was delicious.* But ... you didn't tell me about your troubles caused by the *Financial Times.*"

"Oh, yes. Once, I sat down in my usual place, opened up the *Financial Times*, poked a hole in it and began to look around. I noticed, besides the girls, that some guys in long leather coats kept moving through my field of vision, which was strange because it was ninety degrees in the shade outside. Before long— here they came. They approached me, showed me some kind of ID, and put me in a car."

"Just because you were looking through a hole in a newspaper?"

"No, the charge was much more serious: industrial espionage. You see, across the street from where I was sitting there was a cookie factory. They thought I wanted to figure out the production process and then sell it to a foreign country. Of course, no one is interested in our cookies. It was just an excuse to lock me up."

"Did they torture you?" asked Sandoz.

"No," I replied.

Unfortunately, they did not beat me. It would have been better if they had. I would have taken it better. If there is anything I do not like, it is questions. And they had a lot of questions. They wanted to know as much as possible. I did not know how to answer most of their questions. And so, for hours in the police station, the eternal battle between gnosis and agnosticism went on, in its morose Kali Yuga version, of course. To me personally, those who have the answers to all questions are the most suspect. And, what are *answers*? Oxygen bottles. By using them, you can even breathe at the bottom of a river. But, if someone really exists, they keep their mouth shut. In the last two thousand years, who has heard God speak?

At that instant, the windowpane shattered with a loud crash, and a soccer ball fell into the room. A genuine soccer ball, which had EUROPA CUP printed on it. This incident intensified Sandoz's neurosis. The fans in the nearby stadium were shouting "Give the ball back!" "Hey, faggot!" and "Idiot!" Sandoz was about to grab the glass with the cocktail and gulp it down, but he restrained himself. "I won't give them the ball back," he hissed. In order to calm everything down, although it was hard to do, I referred back to the past and—after who knows how many years—I remembered Jurek, our schoolmate. What a guy! Member of the Literary Club, Math Club, Photo-Cinema Club, Model-making Club and Ham Radio Operators Club. He played soccer, basketball, volleyball, handball, and table tennis for the school teams. On his own initiative, without anyone's help and without any need whatsoever, he removed his sister's appendix during his freshman year of high school. Successfully, nonetheless. The son of a bitch. He carried that *appendix veriformis* around in a jar filled with formalin, and showed it to the girls during lunch break, while we were smoking in the boys' room. Whatever happened to him afterward? Oh, yes. In his sophomore year of high school, he presented a bouquet of flowers to Broz as his excellency was on his way to open a hydro-electric power plant. And what happens to all those who, in one way or another, meet with Broz? Just like Sandoz's platonic sumo wrestler, they attract bad luck. In fact, Jurek graduated from the Colleges of Dentistry, Medicine, Machine Engineering, Mining-Geology, Arts and Sciences, and Forestry. He got a Fulbright scholarship and went to the USA and stayed there. He married and soon after his life ended ignominiously. His wife, as is the custom in America, found a lover, and together they poisoned poor, educated and healthy-as-a-horse Jurek. Radium chloride, I believe. Thus proving that if you do not want to poison yourself, someone else will poison you. Jurek's wife, her name was Barbara, spent three months in jail and then became a rock singer. A mediocre one. I have her only album. But three months for murder, that is really not very long, even if it was just Jurek she murdered. In fact, she did not even serve the full three months. For good behavior, her sentence was shortened to seventy-five days. Scandalous, but lawful. In the American constitution there is a ... An ... I was simply stumped as I searched for the word, so I asked Sandoz.

"Sandoz, that word under twenty-one across in the *Politika* crossword on February 14, 1973. Do you remember what it was?"

"Of course, 'amendment.' Why?"

"Just asking," I said.

And then I thought: amendment. So, there is an amendment which dictates that only symbolic sentences are passed down for the murder of immigrants. And it is justified like this: why did the victim come to America? If he had stayed in his own country, he would not have enticed American citizens to draw their guns or reach for their poison. All laws are disgusting, but this one, at least for me, has some charm to it; if you're going to be killed, it should be in your motherland.

3

And then things finally began to go their natural way: upside-down. Into the room came Sandoz's wife. One of his wives. She started to paint her fingernails. To wiggle her hips. To brush her hair and sing cheap arias from the Top Ten. Things were not looking good. Sandoz started to say something to me, but his wife interrupted him. "Dear, have you seen my glasses anywhere?" "No," barked Sandoz, and he didn't get to tell me what he wanted, or what he seemed to want, because his wife broke in again: "Did you know that Maya called me this morning and told me that . . ." "Hey, that's enough now!" howled Sandoz, who is usually a quiet, civil neurotic. "Haven't I told you hundreds, thousands of times not to interrupt me when I'm talking with my friends? Haven't I?" "Yes," replied his wife. Trembling all over, Sandoz went over to the chest of drawers in the corner, opened a drawer, dumped out a pile of clothes, family photographs, dishes, leather caps, and took out a pistol. I remember it was a Beretta. In spite of the rule that the gun hanging on the wall in the first chapter has to be fired in the third, this gun went off even though I had not noticed it earlier, I had not even known that it existed. His wife theatrically fell to the floor, wounded in the vicinity of her ovaries as far as I, as a layman in anatomy, could tell. She did not bleed much. The gun must have been small caliber. She was not even groaning very loud. I imagined crimes of passion differently, I must admit. It was all rather banal, like most other daily absurdities.

Not even five minutes had passed after the shot rang out, and two policemen showed up in the living room. They said that they heard that a murder had taken place. "Nonsense," Sandoz was calming them down, "that is a bald-faced lie. You boys obviously read too many mystery novels." He tried to explain to them that

he had had a slight altercation with his wife and had accidentally pulled the trigger, that she was only wounded, only slightly at
that, she was hardly bleeding, and as to why she was groaning
and crying for help—that was not even worthy of their attention, that was her professional hang-up, for she was, indeed, an
actress. Sandoz's rhetoric seemed to convince one of the policemen but the other insisted that they stay around a while longer
until they had gathered all the facts. Really, some policemen are
quite smart. But all the others are stupid as became clear to me
momentarily. In the end, the fact that the policemen stayed had
its advantages: at least that way we were safe from the burglars,
rapists, and all the other vagabonds who are wandering around in
these troubled, war-torn times.

Out of politeness, I meandered over to the corpse-to-be of
Sandoz's wife and asked her how she felt. "Bad, really bad," she
said. I offered to get her an aspirin. That was the first thing that
occurred to me. She assented. As I headed toward the bathroom
for the pills, I stopped beside Sandoz. "Isn't it a bit strange that
these policemen showed up so quickly?" I asked in a whisper.
"No," said Sandoz loudly, "it isn't strange at all. These are the
last days. Haven't you ever read René Guénon? He says that at
the end of the world events will happen faster and faster until
the whole thing just flies apart." I'd read Guénon a few years ago,
but in the meantime I'd forgotten what he wrote about. The policemen, I suppose, had not read *Dark Times*, but one of them
showed some curiosity.

"You said 'the last days.' What do you mean exactly? This, of
course, is off the record."

"Kali Yuga. I'll summarize. There are four cosmic cycles: gold-
en, silver, bronze and iron, if I counted them right. Since I've become too dull to explain them, and you've become too dull to
understand, I will make use of a parable. You all know what an
amusement park is. You know. Of course. Well, the golden age,
that is the tunnel of love, the silver is the shooting gallery, the
Bronze Age could be compared with the roller-coaster, and the
Iron Age with the house of mirrors."

While he was talking, the policemen, obviously absentmind-edly, were examining the weapon which Sandoz had shot. Then the doorbell rang. It was a priest. A man dressed in a syncretistic robe, so that he looked like a cross between the pope, a rabbi and a Siberian shaman.

"I was just passing by," said the priest, "when I heard that there was a murder in this house, but that the victim had not died yet, so I thought to myself: I should give her the final con-fession; be there in her time of need."

René Guénon was, it seems, right. News was spreading faster. Especially bad news.

Sandoz was trapped.

"Come on in, father. But I doubt you will be of any help to her. She is, or at least claims to be, a Buddhist. She doesn't believe in God, the holy mystery, and all that."

"To be honest," the priest sighed, "I don't believe it either."

Here, I intervened.

"How can you be a priest then?"

One of the policemen reacted. In a solemn voice, he said that freedom of religious confession was guaranteed by the constitu-tion, and that the priest's right to believe or not was inviolable.

"Gentlemen, gentlemen, please. Everything is all right. I will gladly tell the gentleman, and you all, how I became a servant of the Lord. You see, I graduated in Electrical Engineering, but I simply couldn't find a job. Just about that time, our local priest died, so I passed the supplemental exams and entered the service in his place. I took the job very seriously, even though I am an atheist. If I had gotten a job in my profession, I would not be-lieve in electro-technology either, and I assure you I would still be able to perform as a solid engineer. 'Hey,' I told myself, 'now you're a priest and you will do your best to be a good priest, and to ensure that the souls of your flock go as easily and purely as possible to hell.' I even started looking into theology."

"I want an aspirin!" Sandoz's wife cried out.

"Give that whore an aspirin," cried the priest, "and tell her to stop interrupting me."

One of the policemen obediently fetched the aspirin. In passing, I noticed that he had a symbol on his cap:

This amazed me. It must have been that in the meantime, there outside, the political system had changed. But I did not pay too much attention to that.

"And so," the priest continued pretentiously, "in studying patristics I concluded that all people are more-or-less atheist. This gave me confidence. Here's how. God is so great, surpassing our powers of perception and conception, that no one believes in him to the extent that they can say with certainty 'I believe.' Besides that, we all came from Adam and Eve, and we are therefore necessarily related also to Judas Iscariot, the Marquis de Sade, Hitler, Stalin and to all criminals. They are all our brothers. All of us are, as many of us as there are, bandits, sons-of-bitches, robbers, pimps, scoundrels, and the only thing that can help us is a good upbringing and good manners."

Since, by profession, they are disinterested in theology, the police passed the time while the priest gave his sermon by fiddling with the gun. Even though it did not appear in the first chapter, the gun went off again, thereby ultimately destroying all rules of plot development. The shot, what a coincidence, hit one of the policemen. His colleague stared in shock at the body of his comrade, which was writhing next to Sandoz's wife. When he had pulled himself together a bit, he said: "You are all my witnesses that the gun went off accidentally. I've got such bad luck. Yesterday I fired five rounds at an escaped prisoner and missed all five times, and today I didn't even want to shoot, I didn't even take aim, and I hit my own partner."

"It happens," said the priest.

"But why always to me?"

The wounded policeman and Sandoz's wife cried out in unison:

"Aspirin, we want aspirin!"

Alas, there was no more aspirin. We only found some vitamin C tablets, and these we gave to the wounded, who immediately perked up. The policeman, the one who had accidentally shot his partner, had fallen into a depression. In a moment of despair, he intimated to us that this was the fourth partner he had shot accidentally, and that he had not killed a single criminal in his entire career. His superiors were already beginning to look at him questioningly. It was true that everything had been proven by the commissions, true that there was no shadow of a doubt, but he felt uneasy and was afraid of being suspended. And if in the near future he did not kill a thief—he would commit suicide.

Sandoz comforted him. Rightly so. The wounded policeman was not dead at all; according to the QUALY (Quality Adjusted Life Years) scale, which ranges from 1.0 (completely healthy) to 0.0 (dead), he could be given about 0.3. Nor was Sandoz's wife dead. There was even a chance that they might pull through. But the policeman was inconsolable. He kept repeating over and over: "When I shoot someone—they never get up." He believed this as if it were an axiom.

The shortage of aspirin was becoming alarming. An argument began about who should go shopping. The policeman insisted that he should be the one because he had shot his partner. Sandoz insisted that he should go to the pharmacy because he was the host, and he was the first to draw the weapon. I insisted I should go as a neutral party who had not broken the commandment "*Thou shalt not kill*." The debate was interrupted by the priest. He decided that the policeman should go for the aspirin, and that we should all quiet down so that he could give the dying their last rites. We agreed that the policeman should also buy some iodine, bandages and adhesive strips, because once the shooting starts—experience told us—it is hard to reach a ceasefire agreement.

4

The policeman left to fetch the aspirin. The priest cleared his throat. He took out a notebook of some sort and approached Sandoz's wife. The policeman, he did not even look at. Either he thought that he was a hopeless case or he was only interested in women.

"My daughter," he said in a business-like tone, "your time is almost up. Would you like to confess your sins?"

"I don't know what you're talking about."

"What I mean is for you to recount all the times you lied, stole, killed, or when you were seductive, vile, treacherous . . . Who you screwed, have you had venereal disease, did you mate with animals . . . Did you betray your country and work for foreign intelligence services . . . Did you use public transport without paying . . ."

"I have nothing to say!" she interrupted him.

The priest punched her with his fist. A right cross.

"Maybe that will help refresh your memory."

The woman, semi-conscious from the loss of blood and the blow, broke down into truly rare authentic tears. I could swear that she was not bluffing.

"Sandoz, why is he hitting me, and you're not doing a thing?"

Sandoz shrugged. He was powerless.

"No, my dear. The church is separate from the state. I have no right to mingle in its affairs."

The priest hit her again. An uppercut this time.

"There, you hear? If you don't obey, when the policeman comes back I'll order him to club you with his nightstick. You know I have a contract with the police. Now, have you . . ."

"Yes, I have. I confess it all and I repent. And now I want an aspirin."

But, as we have already said, there was no aspirin. The police-man had gone to the corner drugstore and had not returned yet. There was also no more vitamin C. There was nothing. What else could we expect in a place (if not to use a more pejorative term) where priests work for the police, where words mean the opposite of their dictionary definition, where it is not important who the subject is and who the object is, and where—because of restric-tions—the sequence of tenses is reduced to the present perfect and past perfect? Yes, there is logic in that: the past is not used up as much that way.

Women are talkative by nature and proximity to death means nothing to them. It actually provokes them to talk more. San-doz's wife was no exception.

"So," she said, "the time has come. Just a little longer, and I shall vanish from this world. I am almost not sorry. The little that I mourn is more acting than true mourning. In fact, I no lon-ger wish to see these faces around me. They are only a bit further from death than I although they act as if they were important. They bring me aspirin, give me confessional, worry about the sal-vation of my soul. And this idiot to whom I gave the best years of my youth, even though I didn't love him . . . Moreover, I didn't even want his money . . . And that idiot will not defend me from the attack of a priest who is working for state security. Indeed, I have no reason to mourn."

Then she fell silent. Her pain, obviously, had begun to in-crease. The wounded policeman was also whimpering, which, to a certain extent, went against the belief that policemen are peo-ple without problems and fears. But that was only one in a whole collection of prejudices. Fortunately, his partner, the one who had gone to fetch the aspirin, entered the house beaming, carrying an armload of first-aid supplies. Passing out the medicines and vita-mins, he clarified the reasons for his delay. He said that the phar-macy was crowded, but that he had gotten the aspirin and other things by cutting in line. As he was leaving, he spied the escaped prisoner who had evaded him the day before. He pursued the criminal through three parts of town and as soon as he was in the clear, he had taken a shot—and missed him again. At this point, we weren't sure why he was so happy. So he explained that, too. The bullet which had missed the escaped prisoner struck, though accidentally, a bank robber who was trying to catch a taxi with a bag full of money.

But, the police officer's joy was short lived. Just as he finished telling us what had happened, he fell, struck by a sniper's bullet. The shot had entered silently through the window, most probably from Sarajevo, some 110 miles away from Sandoz's apartment. The technology of war was obviously improving. The priest, as a matter of form, looked for his pulse. He was dead.

"You see how life is nothing," said the wounded partner of the dead policeman. "Just a while ago he was grieving for having shot me, and now he's lying here dead. Before me."

Sandoz heaved a sigh.

"The ways of the Lord are mysterious."

I said:

"The ways of stray bullets are even more mysterious."

"*Pulvis et umbra sumus*," said the priest.

Sandoz's wife began to cry. She told me that, now, no one would arrest Sandoz—one policeman was mortally wounded, and the other was dead—and that his crime would go unpunished. I tried to comfort her; I said that someone else would come, and that even if they did not, Sandoz would turn himself in. While I was so impudently lying (although it would later turn out that I had accidentally told her the truth), the remaining police officer breathed his last. This cheered Sandoz's wife up a bit. The death of others can sometimes be comforting. That was the second death in just one hour.

My gaze inadvertently fell upon the packages of medicine. Each was labeled with the symbol:

5

Sandoz had really been right. Events were unwinding at the speed of film. (A study should be written on the influence of film on the acceleration of time in Kali Yuga.) Not even five minutes had passed since the tragic death of the police officer, and the paramedics rang at the door. I noticed that, on their sleeves, instead of the patch with the red cross, they were wearing the symbol:

They said: "We're here to take the bodies away!" They wanted to take Sandoz's wife away as well, but she protested. She was not dead, she said, she just felt a little weak, but she was already getting better. The paramedics insisted. "We were told that there were three corpses here!" one of them claimed. Soon there will be more than three corpses here. But for now there are only two. So, we sent them outside to wait out the series of events in the margins, so as to avoid additional tension in the already frenetic atmosphere.

Like hell! It is impossible to avoid additional tension. Not in these dark times. As soon as the paramedics had exited, one of the dead policemen walked back into the living room. Alive and well. Obviously in a good mood. This was simply too much. Noticing that we were all taken aback, the policeman asked:

"Gentlemen, I see that my presence here disturbs you. What's wrong?"

"Well, hey," said Sandoz, "just a while ago you were dead. Real dead. A few minutes ago they took you to the morgue."

"God forbid," the policeman smiled, "it is a case of mistaken identity. I am not the one they took away. That was my brother, Valdemar. My name is Kazimir. No, I'm wrong, I am Valdemar, and he was Kazimir. Incidentally we are both policemen, you know, it's a family tradition. There are nine of us brothers and we are all policemen. Actually, I wanted to be a priest, but my father wouldn't hear of it."

"Strange," the priest interjected, "I wanted to be an engineer, and I wound up as a priest. But aren't you saddened by your brother's death?"

"To be honest — no. After all, he fell for his country in the line of duty. And don't forget — there are eight of us left. Now, there was some kind of shooting here, if I was properly informed . . . ?"

"Well," said Sandoz, "if you take . . ."

At this point, the policeman Kazimir or Valdemar, we still weren't sure of his name, looked at his watch and grew serious. And we became serious out of respect for a representative of the law. However, it turned out that in two minutes the latest episode of *Dynasty* was scheduled to air. It astounded me that we could have forgotten that fact. Sandoz quickly turned on the television, and the well-known opening sequence filled the room.

The episode was not one of the better ones. Yet, I had to admit that it was more interesting than the episode which we were all a part of, and we had no idea yet how it would end, but it is tragic, as I said beforehand. In fact, the characters of the show were not doing anything that we had not already done: they were killing each other, taking pills, lying, looking for trouble, pretending that they loved and hated each other. But if someone would've invested hundreds of thousands of dollars into this mess of ours, it would also have been glamorous and interesting. The way things were going, we would have to look for sponsors just to get to the end of our own episode.

"They'll all end up in hell!" cried the priest in an apocalyptic tone.

He most likely meant the characters in *Dynasty*.

"As if we won't?" Sandoz retorted.

The capitalist mentality of Sandoz's wife spoke out. Lying there, pale from the loss of blood, she said that we were a bunch of idiots. She fearlessly defended show business. As if she had read my thoughts, which is not to be excluded because people are often clairvoyant just before they die, she said:

"Listen, if someone would just invest a few million dollars in us, then all of this would make sense. But not like this . . . We drink ersatz coffee, there is no aspirin in the house . . ."

"But what would change, in essence?" inquired the priest.

"Oh," she said teasingly, "many things. We would be wearing nice clothes, living in luxurious homes, we would be mixing nicer drinks."

But everything else would be the same, I thought: absurd, stupid, futile, boring, and tortuous. There is no doubt. Crap is just crap. You can invest billions of dollars—it is to no avail. The structure of the world remains the same. And as more and more money is invested to improve it, it gets worse and worse. Finally, the Christian in me had spoken. Even though I liked the part about the better drinks. I must admit.

Sandoz's wife suddenly took a turn for the worse. She asked for five aspirin, and soon after for the whole bottle, but her pain was increasing. Besides that, things continued, as always, to hurtle in the direction of complete chaos. Without any visible cause, the table lamp fell over with a crash, followed by the bookshelf, the stereo and records, and then one after the other: the china cabinet, the wardrobe, several pictures and finally the chairs. Out of the ashes and dust of this trite Pompeii arose a figure with a camera on his shoulder and a PRESS card stuck in the band of his hat.

"What's this," cried Sandoz, "and who the hell are you?"

"I'm a reporter from the *Evening News*."

"But what are you doing in my house?"

"I'm here to do my job," said the journalist.

In order to make a better impression he took from his wallet a press ID badge and presented it to the policeman. His credentials were in order. We had no idea what was going on: maybe all of this was happening in the offices of the *Evening News*, there was no explanation for it. The journalist, in fact, said that he had been sent by the editor-in-chief, that he was really sorry to bother us, but that he had to complete his assignment like a professional. He even had a work order. And expenses paid. And now, how does one oppose such arguments, the captivating charm of rubber stamps and signatures. Sandoz decided to react anyway. He demanded that the policeman remove the reporter from the apartment.

But the policeman could not.

"I'm sorry," he said, "but there's not a thing I can do here. Freedom of the press is guaranteed. It's the law. For the purpose of better informing the public, journalists are allowed free access to all places."

"I've never heard of that law until now," said Sandoz.

"It was passed recently," explained the policeman. "Journalists are granted the right to investigate whatever happens to cross their minds. They can enter homes, open people's mail, if they have a work order and proper identification, of course. By the way, the law also has an addendum. Namely, journalists, in the interest of any police investigation, must present all data at their disposal for inspection."

While this dispute about the law and freedom of the press was going on, I was reminded of the intriguing symbol which I had dreamed of not long before, and which kept showing up more and more often in public. Even on the reporter's identification card was the triangle with the jagged lightning in the center. What did it mean? The last emblem which I remember, and which is fairly common, was the five-pointed star with its very clear meaning: a heap of trouble. One should be careful with emblems. My friend Era, while meditating over NATO's emblem, supposedly a wind rose, found a swastika hidden in it:

6

Sandoz wanted to clear the air. He asked the reporter what kind of assignment he had been sent to cover at his house, and the guy told him without hesitation that he was here to shoot some photos and write a story about a series of intriguing deaths. We were all shocked. The priest even crossed himself. I thought to myself: where are they now, those who criticized me when I claimed that there is too much freedom in the world? Here, this is what freedom of the press leads to! How could the reporter have known that there was a murder here? That is what Sandoz asked him. The reporter justified himself by saying that his editor-in-chief had told him. Sandoz was persistent: how could the editor have known?

The reporter vacillated.

"Because he thought the whole thing up."

Sandoz grabbed him by the collar. What did he think up? Why did he think it up? It is indeed Kali Yuga, but such things are still impossible; people do not shoot each other on the whim of the editor of a newspaper's crime section. The policeman attempted to separate Sandoz and the reporter, who was constantly repeating lofty statements about freedom of the press. The woman was moaning on the floor. The priest was crossing himself in the corner. I was walking around with my head between my hands. At one point, it seemed that the whole scene, together with us, would explode—so great was the tension—but entropy had its way, and soon we all sat down in the chairs, gasping for air.

The reporter was complaining because his assignment did not say anything about him being a victim as well. Suddenly, everything became too unbearable and I decided to go for a walk. There was danger that the events which occurred in my absence might remain wrapped in the veil of the unknown, but I went out anyway. On the street, it was even more unbearable. I could have expected that. In fact, I did expect it, but I still felt dejected. Men and women, a vast multitude, were walking in all directions, pressing against each other, awkwardly pretending that they were headed somewhere in particular, and for all of that to be at least a little more bearable, another time-space dimension was needed. But that dimension did not appear. In front of a shop window I noticed a family — a father, mother and daughter — as they carefully, almost religiously, observed a jar of jam, a can of beets and a bottle of wine. There was nothing else in the shop window. A divine nation! Hm! I thought: *No pasarán.*

I decided to return to Sandoz's place. Things are always nicer at a friend's house, even when there's a series of mysterious murders in progress. As I might have expected, while I was out, nothing had happened. Just as I opened the door, the action resumed. Sandoz's wife asked the reporter if he had photographed everything. He said that he had. She worried about how she would come out in the photographs, and the reporter told her not to worry about a thing because he was a professional.

"But still, I should have fixed my hair," she said.

"No, no, ma'am, this way it will look more natural."

Sandoz interrupted this frivolous chatter to demand that the reporter explain what he meant when he said that this whole mess had been thought up by his editor-in-chief. The reporter did not object. But in return he asked for a cup of coffee. Sadist that he is, Sandoz ordered his wife, wounded as she was, to go make coffee. For everyone present, at that.

"You see," the reporter began, "it's summer. Everyone is on vacation. Or they are sitting at home pretending to be on vacation. It's boring, and circulation has fallen off. And what can we report on? So the editor-in-chief thinks up an exciting crime, an affair, or something like this here today. I just take the photos and make notes. I have nothing to do with it."

"What do you mean 'he thinks it up,'" asked Sandoz. "A lot of things cross my mind, too, but none of them come true."

The reporter chuckled.

"Yes, but you are not backed by our propaganda machinery and the most modern technology."

Silence fell. Sandoz got upset again. Just in case, I put the gun away in a safe place. "Thought it up how, cooked it up how?" raged Sandoz.

He believed that he was at least in control of his own actions. He still believed only in that, and he was demanding solid evidence. But, according to what the reporter said, he did not understand the organization of the press. For, otherwise, why would he shoot his wife for no reason whatsoever?

"Do you hear what the gentleman is saying, you male chauvinist pig?" moaned the wounded woman as she brought out a tray with cups of coffee on it.

"A man always has a reason to shoot his wife."

"I agree," interjected the policeman, "but he is still liable to criminal charges for doing it."

The reporter took a sip of coffee and went on:

"You see, the press controls 95% of everything that happens in this country. Otherwise, how would news coverage be possible at all? Who would be able to follow all the events, who would write the texts, who would edit them? That's also why newspapers are printed the day before. The texts which are published are, in fact, little prophesies about the next day's events. Besides that, we have obtained the most modern Japanese technology. You have seen the forest of antennas and transmitters on the roof of our skyscraper. You see, although this is not science fiction, those are transmitters which are constantly emitting messages. You, of course, do not hear them, but they etch themselves into your consciousness, and each of us behaves as the editor-in-chief wants us to."

Pure stupidity, I thought. I don't think much of man, but I believe there is probably still a difference between a man and a radio. Or maybe there isn't. Both people and radios babble nonsense. Anyway, on both sides of the media there are people. All that fabulous technology serves only to make cretinism available to everyone—cheaply, efficiently, globally.

"There you have it. Life.," lamented Sandoz. "Half an hour ago we were drinking coffee and discussing dreams, and now we are already in an Orwellian negative utopia."

"Yes, yes," the priest comforted him, "life is nothing, my children. You should pray, pray and only pray. But how can a man pray at all when his prayers are being bugged? You heard what the reporter said. They catch your prayers, tape them, censor them. That which displeases them, they erase and only then do they forward your prayers to God. And God does not like such prayers."

All right, I thought to myself, at least we will be in the papers. Better something than nothing. A little publicity never hurts. At least we can be happy that the press is really free. But only the press.

"Now I've had enough!" cried Sandoz. "I want to be left alone with my wife. All of you go to the other room."

7

Now, I do not know where the others went, but as the chronicler of events I had the right, hidden behind an imaginary curtain, to be present at the parting of two lovers. I am leaving the scenes of tenderness in secrecy, not because I am discrete, but because they are disgusting. I drowned out the shrieks and whispering with nervous attempts to think. There was plenty of reason to panic. From everything the *Evening News* hack had said, only one conclusion could be drawn: the war raging some twenty miles from the scene of these petty events was conjured up at an editorial board meeting. Stop! Aporia. How then can one explain the fact that the circulation of daily papers is on the decline? Easily: because more people watch the news on TV. There is no newspaper capable of transmitting scenes of destruction, murder, slaughter, in such a realistic way and window shoppers in front of barren storefronts need to hold onto the belief that it is still better here . . . Safer . . .

The shrieks in the room got really loud so I cast a glance through the aforementioned curtain. After all, it turns out that all fights, even those culminating in gunfire, end in bed. There was plenty for me to see: Sandoz was lying naked in bed. His wife—with a passion that was hard to imagine due to her physical state—was lashing him with a whip, screaming "*Viva la revolución!*" She had not confessed everything to the priest-engineer after all. Sadistic tendencies, for example. Perhaps poor Sandoz could no longer bear the humiliation and was thus brandishing a revolver. Who knows. The cries died away and the two of them lay beside each other smoking and I almost got sick from it all.

Sandoz, it seems, felt guilty. I concluded this from the fact that he was smoking two cigarettes at once. He even apologized.

"I'm sorry," he said. "I don't know what came over me. I acted a bit rashly. Lately I've been nervous."

"You really didn't have to shoot me."

Sandoz sighed.

"I had no choice. It was stronger than me. Like I was possessed by the devil."

"You could have at least shot me in the leg."

"I was aiming at your leg, but I hit you near the ovaries. You know I am a bad shot. You remember when we went to the amusement park, when B. had just begun to write *The Chinese Letters*, we had just met each other. You wanted me to hit the bull's-eye at the shooting range to get the big teddy bear so that I could give it to you. I shot 1,805 pellets and missed every time."

"How in the world did you manage this time? Do you think it's civilized behavior to shoot your wife?"

Sandoz grew pensive. He became serious.

"What makes you so sure that you are my wife?" he asked.

"What do you mean so sure? I've been living here for twenty years. We sleep in the same room. Sometimes in the same bed. I often give you whippings. Can you deny that?"

Sandoz again became his old self. Irascible.

"No. But that doesn't mean you're my wife. Do you remember our wedding? Do you have a piece of paper with my signature? A signed statement?"

"No," she said. "To be honest, no."

"There, you see."

Again they began to shriek. Fortunately, not out of passion. While they were arguing, their cigarettes had burned down to their fingers and burnt them badly.

The woman did not give up easily.

"Then how is it that we've lived together so long?"

"Um, who knows. I don't even remember if we had children."

"Oh, no, my dear. We had two. Twins. But we drowned them. In the medical lore of the day, the thinking in fashion was that dogs are so resistant and there are so many noble breeds because the first litter is always drowned, so we drowned our first litter."

I thought to myself: maybe that's not a bad idea. All first-borns should be drowned, and that would shorten the agony of this world gone awry. I would have thought some more, but the woman hissed out:

"After all, even if I am not your wife—which I don't care about anyway—that's no reason to shoot me."

Here Sandoz blew up.

"I shot you and—period!"

That woman, that tangle of glands and nonsense, oblivious to the soul she was parasitizing like mistletoe, again raised her voice.

"You're a commonplace coward!"

Sandoz went pale with anger.

"Listen! Stop before I get mad again and find my gun. And, by God, this time I will try to be more accurate. After all, you are a Buddhist. All of this should not be of any importance to you."

"Who says that it is of any importance to me?"

"Then why are you putting on such airs?"

"Because I am afraid," said she. That was the only honest sentence spoken that afternoon, a fragment really, but honest.

"Regardless," she continued, "whether you allow something to be of importance or not, if it is terrible, it will be upsetting and nothing can be done about it."

8

Things got even more complicated. Carrying the book of his fake laws under his arm, reeking of alcohol, Circuit Court Judge Borovski tottered into the room. The policeman immediately stood at attention and the whole situation became official again. Not a trace of black humor, debauchery, or idiocy remained. And behind the judge, a whole retinue of clerks and court executors burst into the room, followed by a crowd of curiosity-seekers and interlopers, without whom no trial is imaginable.

In came the court janitor as well. He hammered a nail into the wall. He hung a picture of the President of the Republic. He went away.

"Mr. Sandoz," said the judge, "these proceedings can . . ."

He did not manage to finish his sentence. Puffing, rushing, as if in some kind of Kankan process, Sandoz's lawyer, Solaya, appeared. Theatrically, as only lawyers can do, he made an objection, if that's what you call it.

"Please, please," he gasped, "things cannot go on this way. My client is not required to give any kind of statement without the presence of the defense attorney."

This was already too much for me, the neutral narrator, so I drew up my courage and spoke out.

"Sir, how did you know that the judge would be here?"

The lawyer looked at me as if I were a complete idiot, which basically I am.

"Sir, the legal system is coordinated. We all work together, but I stopped to have a beer so I'm a bit late."

"Wait," shouted Sandoz, "wait a minute. There is too much coordination. I can't understand a thing."

The judge looked at him very skeptically. Then he asked for a

cold beer. If the accused wants to know something more about
the legal system which is being used to try him, all right, he has
a right to that, but it takes some time, and he, the judge, is really tired. With his foot, Sandoz nudged his wife, who had fallen
unconscious in the meantime, and ordered her to bring the beer.

"You see," began the judge, quite skillfully opening the bottle with a pocket knife, "you are a layman, and I understand that
certain things are perplexing for you. The judiciary, like all other
fields, is constantly being modernized. Moreover, it is being com-
puterized. We no longer leave anything to nature. No longer can
someone just steal whatever they want. There are no more surprise murders . . . hunting for criminals, tortuous pre-trial hear-
ings. The law has been perfected. I'm sure you've read Borges. In
one place he writes that the only map which would be perfect
would be one which corresponded point for point with the territory it represents. As a consequence to that, the conclusion was
reached that a system of law would be perfect only if it contained
both commendations as well as punitive entries for all inhabit-
ants of the state in which the law was valid. And so we've perfected the law. Expanded it. The laws don't just define punishments.
That's old-fashioned. Now the law also assigns crimes to average
citizens and just as there are no two identical people, there are
also no two identical sentences. Each is unique and unrepeatable.
And not only does the law predetermine who the offender of the
crime will be—it goes even further—it also indicates the time
and place of the crime. In this way, great savings are made in the
national budget. This hack (he indicated the reporter) perhaps
told you that everything is determined in the editorial offices of
newspapers. That is nothing but common nonsense. They overes-
timate their importance. The newspapers are just an organ of the
Socialist Union of Working People, and nothing more."

The judge took a healthy swig of beer and belched. This is the
New World Order, I thought. Then the judge went on babbling.

"Of course, everyone thinks it's a privilege to be a judge. I'm
not complaining, but it's not easy for me. Sometimes I envy those
judges of the old school who sat in their comfortable chairs,

wrapped in togas, idly napping. Anyway, I wanted to be a soccer referee; I even finished the training school and got my license from FIFA, but since I was a bit overweight (and the law here is clear: a referee cannot weigh more than 160 pounds) I had to finish law school and do this responsible and thankless job."

Lord knows how long the tipsy judge would have gone on casting pearls had he not been interrupted by the priest, who had been wrapped in the opaque darkness of textual oblivion till then.

"If it's not indiscreet of me to ask, I would like to know on the basis of what criterion is it decided who will be a thief, who a murderer, who a robber?"

"It's based on a random sample of the population," the judge said.

"I must admit, that's not just."

"Since when is crime just?"

How could such an argument be opposed? One of the troubles of this world is that the greatest filth and most loathsome of malice are logical, well-argued, and scientifically well-founded, while it is almost impossible to substantiate that which is beautiful.

The priest, however, did not give up so easily. As he had said—although he was an engineer by education—he did his duty conscientiously.

"Of course crime is unjust. But don't you ask yourselves: perhaps among those randomly selected thieves and criminals, there are also those who do not want to be criminals?"

"No one wants to be a criminal. That's first. Second, and as a priest you should know this, all people are sinners and all are potential criminals. Offenders, after all, are chosen by computer. Abuse of the system is impossible."

And then, when we least expected it, Sandoz's wife breathed her last. Without a trace of theatrics. That fact might have even gone unnoticed had the paramedics not come in with the stretcher, and this time she could not protest.

Inadvertently I glanced at the Legal Code which the judge had placed on the table.

On its cover was the symbol:

9

The court janitor brought in some aspirin. It was evident that our supply was running out, and that the twenty pills left would not be enough to deal with the imminent headaches. So, we drew straws to see who would run to the pharmacy to buy more. The lucky one, by unwritten law, was again the policeman. The trial could begin. The judge routinely charged Sandoz with the murder of his wife. The lawyer objected: the murdered woman was not Sandoz's wife; they lived in a common-law marriage, and there are indications that they were only accidental acquaintances. The objection was sustained and accepted as a mitigating circumstance. And now came my five minutes in the spotlight. I was supposed to testify. Everyone who has read the second chapter of this account knows that I do not like to answer questions. That I do not know how to answer questions. Especially official ones. The judge knew this as well. But nothing could be done about it. Justice must be served.

"So," I said, "this is what happened. Today, about two in the afternoon, I came here for my regular visit with my friend. We were drinking coffee and talking . . ."

"What about?"

"About nothing important. About little things. As I was saying, we were chatting, and then, suddenly, into the room came the deceased. In a negligee. Wearing garish make up. She was constantly interrupting us, interrupting Sandoz with all sorts of interjections, undermining his political convictions. I must emphasize that I had never seen her before today. What kind of relationship she had with my friend, I do not know. That, after all, is not even important. I must say that Sandoz warned her several times not to disturb us, but the victim did not take heed. And then, obvi-

ously in a fit of derangement, Sandoz shot her. Then the policemen arrived."

They say, when all is said and done, synchronicity does not
exist. But at the very instant when I uttered the phrase "then the
policemen arrived," Valdemar, no, Kazimir, came in with an armload of aspirin. He was beaming with happiness—a truly rare
occurrence in these gloomy times of war. We soon discovered the
reason for his satisfaction. Namely, as he was leaving the pharmacy he saw the escaped convict that his deceased brother, may he
rest in peace, had so fruitlessly chased. He was trying to steal an
old lady's wallet.

"I shouted: Halt! He took off running. I chased him, fired a
shot, then a second, then a third and—pow—right in the back
of the head."

Justice, they say, is slow but certain.

We could all breathe easier, we had enough aspirin to go
around. Judge Borovski, now visibly tipsy, continued with his or-
chestrated trial. For the crime which Sandoz had committed, the
strictest of sentences was prescribed: death by firing squad. There
was no doubt that the judge would hand down the sentence; perhaps even carry it out personally. The lawyer did his best, within the bounds allowed for employees of the state. He objected
again. His objection was essentially this: wouldn't the deceased
have died sooner or later even if Sandoz had not shot her? If so,
then it was absurd to accuse a man of something which would
happen anyway by the very nature of things. The judge did not
object too much to this. From a philosophical perspective, he
believed that it was indeed absurd, inhuman and irreconcilable
with the humanistic stance of our society. However, seen from a
legal standpoint, and he was a judge, things were different.

The priest also tried to intervene on Sandoz's behalf. That was,
after all, also his duty. Priests should be misogynists and should
take the man's side. One woman plus or minus, that means nothing. He quoted the Bible. "Vengeance is mine, thus sayeth the
Lord." Judge Borovski did not take issue, commenting that, in
our country, the church was independent, but separate. Drink-

ing up yet another bottle of beer, he showed a certain sympathy for Sandoz. He said that deep down he did not blame him at all. The dice could have, he said, landed on his own number. And he could have shot his wife. Actually, he would have done so quite readily. But, justice must be served. And then he gave Sandoz the death sentence.

The lawyer, despite the fact that he had been bribed and was in collusion with the judge, was actually not that stupid. Truth be told, death sentences are tautologies. We are all condemned to death in advance. What kind of satisfaction can be taken in the formal confirmation of that fact and in its violent implementation? I cannot explain it other than to say that it is a part of the project of making man equal to God.

Yet, the death penalty was hanging over me as well. Although I was not expecting it, the judge accused me of being an accomplice. Most unjustly, judging from what I wrote about the event, but it is always possible that I had left something out, and the judge wanted to clear up the case completely. I have to admit, I felt uncomfortable. More uncomfortable than usual. But, at the same time, I ruminated on the aporia: why does life become dear, even more so, when it is senseless and difficult? Ultimately, whether killed by a firing squad, shot by Judge Borovski or hit by a sniper's bullet in a civil war—what is the difference? The state always finds a way to liquidate its subjects. That is the reason it exists, after all.

In spite of everything, I did not give up. I stated firmly that I just happened to be in Sandoz's house, and that I saw no reason why I should be held responsible for his actions. "You don't see the reason!" shouted the judge. "Then you are either blind or you are playing dumb. Sandoz accidentally shot his wife. If you do not understand that, you do not understand the essence of the system. Everything is accidental and nothing is accidental, when seen from a legal standpoint. And since you do not have a lawyer, you can use Sandoz's. He will not need him anymore anyway."

The charge against me was summed up like this: if I had not come to visit Sandoz, things would have gone in a completely

different direction. This logic didn't make sense to me but I didn't
want to insist on explanations, luckily the judge stopped to clari-
fy. Obviously, he had figured out that there were two more beers
in Sandoz's refrigerator, so he was trying to draw the trial out as
long as possible. Yes, the offenders were determined by the State
Computer; on first examination this had nothing to do with me,
but my arrival had disturbed the flow of events. The defense attorney intervened. Tepidly. Just to defend the honor of his profession. Even though he was a real bastard, he was a professional.
The judge paid absolutely no attention to his infrasonic pro-
tests. He accused me of not doing anything to stop Sandoz from
shooting his wife. Why should I stop him? I never liked to get involved in the intimacies of married couples. But, I saw that my
defense was in vain, and that the judge was spinning the threads
of a charge that only made sense because they were being spun by
a man whose blood alcohol content was spiraling upward at an
astronomical rate.

10

In truth, I was being sentenced for political reasons. But in order to maintain the national democratic image and positive world opinion, the state set up the death of a third-rate actress so that I could be charged as accomplice to her monstrous murder. Behind the whole setup, I saw the workings of the structuralists, the literary critics and the post-modernists. Using the troubled times of the civil war, they had decided to capitalize on the blood-thirstiness of the regime and get rid of me, as revenge for all the insults I had generously doled out on them in the tabloid press both here at home and abroad.

If I am not mistaken, structuralism appeared here at the end of the 70s. At first it was just an outdated intellectual trend, but it would ultimately cause a string of strange and dangerous events. At that time practically all periodicals here published series of thematic editions dedicated to the movement. Many famous and not-so-famous structuralists visited Belgrade, held lectures, went barhopping, and took young female students of world literature to their rooms in luxurious hotels to make little structuralists. Up until then, Yugoslavia was a rather pleasant, cozy little nook. The Ruler was still alive and firm in his decision never to die; time was marching on in a straight line; the sale of smoked meat products was on the rise; the birth rate was satisfactory; and the Mutiny on the Bounty had long since been squelched with blood.

And then, slowly at first, things started downhill. The Butterfly Effect. The subversion of deconstruction and countless tirades about decoding caused the first tectonic shifts in the depths of our, ever unstable and collective, unconscious. The most foreboding of omens was the Ruler's illness. You have to admit it: he struggled heartily against newfangled western things, he held

marathon negotiations with death. Not realizing that this farce
had been set up by the structuralists — magnanimously using the
scholarships financed by his very own government — he blamed
his mortality on a coalition of domestic and foreign enemies who
were supported by the money of international reactionaries. Although he could never have dreamed of it, the Ruler became a
structuralist. The later research of Dr. R. Hamsun of the University of Uppsala leaves no doubt about that. According to Dr.
Hamsun, the Ruler had been so decoded already by 1950 that he
had ceased to be a human being and had become a symbol. The
same author claims that the Ruler would never have died if the
deconstructionists had not interfered.

The events of that time are shrouded in darkness. In the first
place, the Ruler's name TITO was nothing more than an ana-
gram (one of the favorite tricks of black magic priests) for the
Egyptian divinity TOTH and the German word TOT — dead.
Translated into everyday terms, the Ruler had been dead long before his date of death, and his death anticipated the huge number of deaths which would be caused later by the war.* Like those
who completely lose their soul and continue to "live" for a time
because they do not go to hell, but rather are condemned to complete nothingness, Josip Broz Tito spent exactly thirty more years
on the earth hunting, fishing, traveling around, firing his clos-
est advisers, opening factories and new highways, drinking whiskey and wine spritzers and being involved in all the other activ-
ities, quandaries, difficulties, and privileges which the duties of
the head of state entail.

Another important feature of the Ruler's loyalty to structuralism was the language he used to express himself. The strange
mixture was (according to Dr. Hamsun) a twisted slang of the
proto-language used by the builders of the tower of Babel, simultaneously understandable and incomprehensible, with which he
managed to talk for hours without saying a thing. The very lan-

---

* I saw Tito once. It was in 1967 in Užice, when he was passing through to open the
Bajina Bašta hydroelectric power plant. Just for an instant I saw him through the window
of his car. He was all bronze and had already started to look like many of the statues and
busts of him scattered across Yugoslavia. In 1992, I tried, using a cabalistic method, to
breathe life into the bronze monument to him which had been moved behind the museum
in Užice. I did not succeed.

guage, the doctor claims, which will be used just before the end of the world. But let's set aside linguistics and eschatology for now. The country which the Ruler was governing was occupied by deconstructionists. Not out of cupidity, but because they wanted to destroy it. They used it as an experiment which would ultimately divulge the method for destroying the rest of the world. Isn't this obvious from the entire pseudo-heraldry of its trite emblem: six torches which symbolize the fire of the sixth circle of hell, in which a significant number of the country's subjects will burn, and a banner with the date 11.29.1943, which contains two of the most evil of numbers (cf. Chevalier: *Dictionary of Symbols*)?

It is also interesting that the Ruler died in Ljubljana, the capital of the republic which would give the *coup de grace* to a country that had already been fundamentally deconstructed. To be more precise, *died* is too strong a word. He disappeared, faded away, evaporated, and all that was left on the hospital sheets was a stain. This put a lot of generals, janitors and various members of various committees in a rather uncomfortable position. Primarily because such a phenomenon was against their Marxist convictions, and secondarily because it was impossible to embalm *nothing* and display it in the grandiose mausoleum which was, cloaked in the greatest of secrecy, designed by the architect B. Bogdanović. The problem was solved by putting a wax figure in the coffin, a true rendition of the Ruler, done in the workshops of Madame Tussauds Museum.

On the Ruler's tomb, on the outside, there are no symbols whatsoever. On the inside, however, writes Dr. Hamsun, a symbol is carved into the marble about which he knows nothing at all, and it looks like this:

11

Yet, by what means had I so begrudged the structuralists and the state bureaucracy? Was it perhaps because I had published *The Atlas of Non-Existing Countries*, in which I'd included the Socialist Republic of Yugoslavia as a significant regional power, placing it on the borders with Neverland, Palestine, Tlön, Uqbar, Utopia and Shangri-La. Only Gottfried Rosenkreutz could know that. But who is Gottfried Rosenkreutz? That question is not easily answered. Especially not with the charge of accomplice to a horrible murder hanging around one's neck. Perhaps it is not possible to answer the question at all. Maybe it is not possible to talk about Rosenkreutz at all. But how can one not talk about it when it is fashionable? About his identity, constant debates are being held in the circles of the pseudo-esoterics, structuralists and agents of the secret services. The dossier carrying his name is growing thicker and thicker, and the unknown facts and uncertainties about Rosenkreutz are ever greater and more vague. Strangely, his works are readily available and are even popular. They have been translated into several languages, but no one has ever actually seen the author. I envy him on that account. The few facts available about him are fabrications; there is not even a grain of truth to them. And yet, that means nothing.

Contrary to popular opinion, the truth is not the truth. It is only a skillfully constructed lie. Just as it is with people; some are to be believed, some are not. Rosenkreutz himself reflected on that. In his work *Theology for Atheists*, he wrote these words: "The only truth is God. Therefore nothing. Everything which is *something* contains at least 95% lies."

He almost won the Nobel Prize for the aforementioned book. They say that he lost it only because the conservatives of the Swedish Royal Academy did not want to award it to a person of such questionable existence. The criteria of academicians are strange. Tolstoy existed big time, and what is more, he cared about existing and about awards, but he got the short end of the stick. Injustice is equally divided on both sides of the line which separates those whose existence has been confirmed, and those whose existence cannot be established.

Indeed, who is Rosenkreutz? The pseudonym of a real person or pseudo-person with a real name? I would never have started researching him if I had not been trying to stop smoking. Since that was impossible for me, I had to work on something impossible. I paced wildly about the room and dictated to a black man who I had hired for a pittance to scribble instead of me. Being so nervous, I shouted at him: "Damn it, where is Rosenkreutz?" I shouldn't have shouted, it's not my style, but I wanted to upset the leftists and the humanist intelligentsia! Now I was paying dearly for it.

Thus, the question I have asked who knows how many times: Who was Gottfried Rosenkreutz? Certainly not a German. As pedantic as they are, the Germans would have found his trail long ago and destroyed every mention of him if they had found that he did not exist. Germanic discipline does not allow such flexibility on questions of identity. You either are, or you are not. Not like it is in this country. And that's all right. After all, I never would have become interested in that gifted, though wily, adventurer, had I not quit smoking. And then started again out of nervousness.

To make the irony greater, it seems that Rosenkreutz is a heavy smoker. In one source I uncovered the fact that it was actually Rosenkreutz who had brought tobacco from Europe to America, where about a hundred years later the conquistadors found it and brought it back. Chronologically this is untenable, but is Rosenkreutz tenable? Is anything tenable? After all, if someone exists to such a small degree, hardly noticeable, what is the difference *whether they live now or they lived two thousand years ago?* His first book has its origins in that time. It is entitled *On the Multitude of Strange Plants Which Grow in India and Their Influence on People's Health.* His name is mentioned even before that. As far back as ancient Greece. A scroll was found (it is kept in the British Museum) in which, among the fragments of a text on narcotics used for the Dionysian mysteries, it is clearly written "... just as Rosenkreutz taught."

Fine. I can come to a simple conclusion: Rosenkreutz is a pseudonym. Simply a pseudonym. Perhaps this could even be logically supported with the help of representatives from the Socialist Party of Serbia. Just how many people are there on earth who have never authored a book? So why couldn't there be just as many books which have no author? But this would violate the Law Against Free Speech so the local censors just say that the book was authored by Gottfried Rosenkreutz. Like hell! As we will see, Rosenkreutz kept meticulous records. There are letters, personal items, photographs. Even though it was a pseudonym, a birth record appears for Gottfried Rosenkreutz, but there is not a trace of who he really was. His name appears everywhere, even when it is impossible, unacceptable, absurd. Is he being persecuted? Not very likely. None of his books have been outlawed. And then again, who knows?

Rosenkreutz's bibliography is actually not very long. Several tracts, articles, two or three books, thirty poems. It could hardly be very large. Rosenkreutz is always on the move. Like a shark. More precisely: like the ghost of a shark. In a formal-legal sense, he is nonsense and that is why he is doing so well. You cannot bring charges on the basis of literary texts or gossip in bars. Not even Circuit Court Judge Borovski can do that.

The final question: am I not Gottfried Rosenkreutz, perhaps? Impossible. That idea has grown stale. All a researcher has to do is go to the Boomerang Café and have a look in THE TIBETAN BOOK OF THE DEAD DRUNK where, under the entry for B he will find a pile of documents about what I drank and said, with whom I sat and when. Along with the rest of the nebulous facts gathered. That is how history is made. The researcher can take that book, actually it is a grease-smeared folder, and place it next to the Helsinki Accord to see if there is any connection, and surely there is, scholarship claims, although I doubt the possibility: everything is chaos. And the more order we try to introduce into the confusion, the greater the chaos becomes.

But for the confusion to be absolute, as is appropriate, it will be proven that Rosenkreutz (while I was drinking coffee with Sandoz on the evening of the murder) showed up at the Boomerang Café. He drank: rum, whiskey, vodka, vinjak, brandy, schnapps, calvados, rum, cognac, schnapps, wine, beer, Irish coffee, cocktails, champagne and liqueur. On my bill at that. Thus he will say: "I am Rosenkreutz." He introduced himself and showed those present a cane with a gold-plated handle, a gift from Salvador Dalí. He signed the bill. That's the trouble, the eternal trouble with history. How difficult it is to write a credible account of a drinking binge in a small bar in the Balkans. Or about anything else, for that matter. Wherever you look—forgeries. Unreliable witnesses. Perjurers.

Thus, Rosenkreutz appeared, left an impression and then departed. They watched him leave. With Dali's cane he parted a sea of puddles like Moses, and went the way of the Promised Land, to the Canaan of inauthenticity, unreliability, and unverifiability.

12

These digressions did not help me. Borovski was ruthless. The sentence was pronounced: death by firing squad. The lawyer, for the sake of form, again protested. He thought the sentence too harsh. The judge did not agree. Evidently he had had enough. He wanted to go home as soon as possible to get some rest. After all, he justified to himself, he did not write the criminal code, but if the honorable lawyer believed the punishment to be excessive, he had the right to appeal. It turned out the procedure was the following: he had to appeal, at that moment, orally, to Borovski. The lawyer did so. He requested that the death sentence be overturned and replaced by a misdemeanor sentence.

"In principle," said the judge, "that is not impossible, but the appeal is rejected."

The lawyer asked for an explanation. It was a banal one. Punishments for misdemeanors were monetary. With inflation so high, by the time they are paid they become worthless, and thus lose all effectiveness in reforming the convicted person.

The judge asked for some coffee. But who would make coffee? Sandoz's wife had died. The policeman—Valdemar or Kazimir—offered his services. He went to the kitchen. The judge studied us, all bloated and official.

"Gentlemen, gentlemen. Why all the gloominess? You keep saying how banal, boring, awful, absurd, and worthless life is, and now you're sad."

The fact is that life is just like that. But Sandoz and I both secretly doubted that death was much better either. Rightly so. The priest advised us to seek comfort in religion. But Sandoz, skeptic that he is, said that religion is the opiate of the masses. What's wrong with opium, I asked aloud. The judge jerked up out of his lethargy.

"Please. The right to religious confession is guaranteed by the constitution, but trafficking in narcotics is a criminal act."

Would they shoot us twice if by chance there was some opium and we smoked a pipe or two in order to ease our suffering? No, but, the law dictates that opium users should have their right hand cut off before they are executed. So, we lit a cigarette. That was still allowed. But not for long, not for long.

Then came another unpleasant surprise. The reporter asked the judge when the sentence would be carried out. To everyone's surprise, Borovski showed remarkable efficiency: we were to be shot as soon as he finished his beer. It was the last bottle of beer Sandoz had in his refrigerator. To make things more interesting, the execution was to take place right there. It was more humane that way, the judge observed. The days of the barbaric loss of life in dank cellars, in nasty rooms, are over. Now it is done in a domestic atmosphere. That is another one of the innovations to the judiciary system.

"But it has its downside, too," the judge said.

"Today, for example, I sentenced a witch to be burned at the stake. While the sentence was being carried out, the fire spread to the building next door, and the fire department had to be called in. It was really unpleasant for me. I thought that witches were no longer burned. But they are. In fact, very rarely. The last time was, if my memory doesn't fail me, in 1783. But the evidence against this one was incontrovertible. I had no choice."

The policeman brought in the coffee.

The proceedings were to occur in the following order: after we drank our coffee, we would move on to the death penalty. The firing squad was present in the form of the policeman. By very fortunate circumstances, the priest was there also. Before they shot us, we had the right to a last request. Sandoz asked for a steel-blue Porsche GT. That was out of the question; anyway the stores were closed. I decided to be clever. My last wish was for Judge Borovski to tell us about an especially interesting case from his experience as a judge.

It worked.

"Well, if I really must. There is a whole anthology of such stories, but I will choose one particularly instructive case which will serve you as an illustration of the complexity of my job. So, one day a man who liked to listen to loud music left his apartment and forgot to turn off his stereo. This man had a neighbor who usually took a nap in the afternoon. This particular afternoon, because of the loud music, he could not go to sleep, so he went outside. These are our rights as citizens. True, but the neighbor, the one who couldn't sleep, met a friend in the street whom he hadn't seen since their thirtieth high school reunion. And instead of going home as he had intended, he got in the car with his friend and they went to a bar on the outskirts of town. They made themselves comfortable. They ordered a bottle of wine. And then another. And then another . . . And so, our friend was drinking with his school buddy, and meanwhile his wife, in a state of derangement turned on the gas in the apartment. Precious minutes slipped by, and the husband did not return home at the usual time. It was already too late for anything to be done. Dizzy from the gas, the woman could not manage to call the emergency response services. Soon she died. Because of a stereo left on.

"Not till around midnight did the inebriated friends leave the bar. At an intersection, drunk as they were, they ran over an unsuspecting locomotive engineer who was on his way to work. The locomotive engineer, crippled for life, was taken to the hospital with a broken back. His fiancée later left him. Not that night, no, but still, one marriage less, at least three sons less, three soldiers less for our army—all of that went to hell because of a stereo left on. But that is not the end of the misfortune. Due to the engineer's accident they had to find a replacement; therefore the train was delayed and because of the delay it ran into a freight train. The toll: eighty-seven dead, two hundred fifty lightly or seriously wounded.

"There was no end to the accidents. One of the travelers who had changed his mind about getting on the train because it was late, went mad with happiness because he wasn't on the train;

he took a rifle, climbed to the top of a tall building and began randomly shooting passersby. In doing so, he killed twenty-five people. The police surrounded the building. In the confrontation with the maniac, four policemen were killed. Then a police sniper finally shot the maniac.

"But that's not all. Being a sensitive person, realizing that he had killed a man, the sniper left the police force, got involved in drug dealing and began to sell heroin in front of a high school. Misfortune always displays a tendency to expand. Just by accident, among the twenty-five killed by the maniac there were eight Arabs. Arab terrorists, thinking it was a setup by the Mossad, returned the blow which they had not actually been dealt. They put a bomb in an airport building. Toll: eighty dead. And what is more, God got angry, and in order to punish the spread of cosmic chaos, he caused an earthquake in Iran. You all know: there were about fifty thousand casualties. And all of that because of one irresponsible citizen who didn't turn off his stereo."

"Was he at least punished for it?" asked the priest.

The judge sighed.

"Unfortunately not. He is still at large."

13

The policeman began to check his gun. Judge Borovski asked for an aspirin. He had had a long day. Like all of us, for that matter. And the priest and the reporter also had terrible headaches. The policeman also got a headache, out of solidarity with the representative of the judiciary. Thank God, there were plenty of aspirin. They all took two at once.

Sandoz had a headache, too. My head felt like it was about to explode. But, was there any point in taking pills against pain at such a moment?

The judge filled out the forms for the sentence.

And then something interesting happened. All at once, they all grew pale. Heavy beads of sweat broke out on their foreheads. Their hands began to shake. Sandoz looked at me. I had no idea what was going on. And then my gaze fell on the medicine bottle. Instead of *Aspirin*, it said *Strychnine*. The policeman, it seemed, had bought poison by mistake. Or had the lady at the pharmacy made the mistake? This will be uncovered by some other judge and he will tell it to his future sentencees just before passing judgment, as Sandoz and I are still at large.

I have to admit, the scene was tortuous. They writhed about on the floor and screamed so loudly that we had to turn the stereo up full blast so as not to disturb the neighbors. Yet, all in all, the agony did not last that long. Perhaps about fifteen minutes. Then everything quieted down.

When a judge dies, the statute of limitations runs out. This, at least, is a known fact. We could breathe easy. But we did not.

Out of the gloom, sooty, bloody, and ragged from a hard day's work, the hospital attendants appeared with a stretcher. The priest, judge, reporter and policeman rounded it out to 2,500 deaths which had been set as the daily quota for this war. Darkness could descend at last.

Lost in the Supermarket

I got lost in the supermarket. I wanted to buy something, some little thing; I was walking for a long time through the labyrinth made by the shelves of products, and suddenly I realized that I was lost and that I would never again find my way to the exit. It was about five to eight, I was on page XX, the store was closing at eight, the chances I would reach the exit were equal to zero. What could I do? I sat down on *SOMETHING*, it was crooked so I'm writing it in *italics*, I sighed and buried my face in my hands. I think I went into the supermarket to buy a couple of SUPER SILVER razor blades. I needed to shave. Or to cut my wrists. It would be more honest to say that I wanted to cut my wrists, because I was already cleanly shaved. I stood up and straightened out the *SOMETHING* I was sitting on, so that now it was SOMETHING. I can do nothing more for myself. I will sit on SOMETHING until the end of the story. But I cannot just sit here in silence. I need to talk about something, otherwise there will be no story. Bob Horn, disguised as a woman, told me that I should talk about something in the story LOST IN THE SUPER-MARKET. But I just can't remember what. If I fall silent, that's the end of the story. I cannot believe that we're at the end, I cannot believe that the short-story collection will end in the supermarket. At 8:20. The clock showed me unambiguously that it was 8:20; it spread its hands safely, high up on the wall, grinning at me and showing me its *8:20*. I didn't believe it. How can you believe an apparatus that repeats the same story day after day at the same tempo. No, I thought, I will never again trust such an unreliable apparatus. Something which repeats itself, something so inconstant, I refuse to trust it. Because the bastard that one minute before was claiming that it was 8:20, suddenly started to claim something else: *8:21*. The clock, so it seemed, noticed that I

had seen through its dirty game. It started ticking more quietly. It
didn't stop. I'll bet it was scheming: time is on my side; sooner or
later I'll break him. But such calculations were wrong. I had seen
through clocks once and for all: they only measure the length of
their senseless tick-tocking. There is no time there whatsoever.
Time is, after all, someone's idée fixe, a presupposition which has
been going on *for centuries*. Suddenly I felt an incomprehensible
hatred toward the clock. "You and those like you have divided
my life into years, months, weeks, days, hours, minutes and seconds. You've split everything up, destroyed it, shattered it. Too
long did I believe you. Too long did I live in error. I might fairly well believe in *now*, but in the past and future, no way! Those
are grammatical categories. It's fine if you get along better in your
phantom-like time but I get along better in space. I will destroy
you! I'll break you into pieces! I'll stop you once and for all!"
But my anger quickly subsided. How could I go against the millions of clocks? They are, after all, just tools. The real culprit is
unknown. Again I sat down on SOMETHING, sighed and buried my face in my hands. What would my mom say if she saw
me now, shouting at clocks? I felt miserable. Did the clock hate
me back? We looked at each other, face to face. Equally nonsensical. Both of us victims. The clock kept claiming that time was
passing, the hands kept showing something different. Every thirty seconds or so, approximately, a single tear would appear in the
corner of my eye, only to slide down my cheek and shatter on the
dirty floor of the supermarket.

Just as I reached page eighty-one, the telephone rang. At
first I didn't want to answer. Why should I answer? It was not
my number. Somebody had probably dialed the wrong number. Who would call the supermarket at this hour? But the telephone rang rang and rang until it finally convinced me that *someone* knew that I was in the supermarket and wanted to talk with
me. I picked up the receiver, afraid that *Calcium Sandoz*, upon
reading these lines, would say, "It's too much like Kafka." "This is
God," the voice in the receiver said, "I want to talk to you." The
voice came through from a long distance and it was *indescribable*.

Perhaps someone is lying about their identity, I thought. But who? Only God knew that I was lost in the supermarket. "Lord," I said, "why are you calling me? Why are you tempting me?" "What were you expecting?" asked God. "You want us to talk face to face?" I realized that I had messed up, that I had been arrogant and stupid. And yet, I wasn't the worst. There are those who are more arrogant than me. My mom and Dr. Wong, for example. If they were here, they would say I'd gone crazy and was talking with a telephone receiver. "I see," the Lord began again, "that you have some complaints about time. You're irritated by clocks. In fact, you're desperate, and you're desperate because you're the worst. I created time, long ago now, not to make things pass through it just for the sake of nothing, but so that transience would be noticed and people would turn to the eternal. But what are you doing? You're grasping at the tatters of events, and despairing because they disappear. You write books about it. Short books, of questionable value, but still books. You say that you can never get over a couple of people's departures from your life. That's because you're arrogant and selfish. Satan fell for the same reason. Don't forget that fact. You write that you believe in me; that's why I'm calling; you're constantly mentioning me, and you're only important to yourself. And you won't forgive anyone! You act like me. Only you're incomparably more imposing. Come, O poet, admit it: you've never loved anyone! You place yourself in the center of the world, you accept this fellow or that one only as much as they admire you, and you call this malicious inclination to adore you 'love.' Unpleasant, O poet, isn't it? But just remember: the horror that overcame you every time someone you loved departed did not arise from the feeling that you'd lost something you loved—love is incompatible with horror— rather, you suffered because you felt you were no longer an idol at whose feet sacrifices would be laid. You ran away to China to escape my wrath; you thought: in China, there is officially no God, nobody will be able to touch me there. But I am who I am. I am omnipresent. Think about your life a little bit! Go back into the past a bit! Don't trust in phantoms. For your information, I do not have a very high opinion of your prose. I don't care much for prose anyway, but my opinion of yours is exceptionally negative because it is full of lies and cowardice. You conjured up a Fin and a Tmu and then you filled their mouths with words that you wouldn't dare say yourself. So! That will be all. Don't forget, I forgive only those who forgive others." God slammed down the receiver. He didn't leave me a phone number. Secretly, I had so longed to hear His Voice, and then what I heard totally stunned me. I sat there like an idiot on SOMETHING, sighing and burying my face in my hands. Is it possible that I'm like that? I used to think that I didn't have the best opinion of myself. And I don't. I had created a negative opinion of myself, a poor self-image, which might even have been endearing. My real *self* I hid somewhere in the depths, from where all that intolerance and hatred gushes forth. In the meantime, my SOMETHING went crooked and became *SOMETHING* again. I straightened it out. That was all I could do for myself. What more can a man do, a man at whom has had the truth of the Lord God thrown in his face?

I know how Sisyphus felt. As soon as one paragraph is finished, as soon as a period is put at the end of the last sentence, a new paragraph appears, surfacing like a nightmare out of the whiteness of the page. I didn't need this at all. I almost avoided all this trouble, almost evaded the whole mess, so I could laugh at the whole circus from a safe distance. I wanted, truth be told, to end my relationship with the world. I was young then, full of strength, or rather full of nausea. I didn't want to go on just talking to the appearances of people and the surfaces of things. I thought that the parting would be much easier, that I would simply turn my back on appearances, like a pouting child; I supposed: I'll wave my hand carelessly and soon all the tumult will cease, the alternation of day and night; I hoped the lies would finally shut up and that the rain would never fall again. But things got quite complicated. It turned out that I was more caught up in pretty lies, in little things, than I had guessed not so long ago when we made the decision that each of us should go his own way: the world should go with the ebb and flow of its [own] history,

I should go somewhere else or nowhere, so that I could finally *be born*. I didn't hesitate. Our parting was final. The whole thing was ruined by small, actually tiny, little things. I didn't pay attention to those little things until I wrote a couple of stories with Bob Horn in them; he turned my attention to the fact that I would write about them one day in *this story* which I am writing under horrendous circumstances. But then it was already too late. And even more than that. I was going to take that last decisive step, I tell you; I had taken a deep breath and prepared myself, and then the little things, the knickknacks, began to make me feel pity, to force me to hold back my tears. It's easy enough to part with the world generally speaking—this is for those of you who would like to clear things up with the world—but it is much more difficult to deal with the fine details. My pocketknife for example. I've had it for years! I myself don't know how I never lost it. All that time I either took it with me, or not, I never really thought about it, I couldn't even really use it to cut my wrists, and then, at the moment of truth when I was supposed to throw it away so that nothing more would tie me to the past, I took it in my hand and hesitated for a while, and then put it back in my pocket. I could not part with that dead object. I'll never throw it away. I know that now. If it wishes me well, the knife will have to try to disappear on its own. I will not lift a finger; I, the sentimental old fool who has gotten lost in the supermarket and still believes a little in love. The knife told me so. Not in the way we tell each other stupid things. In the way in which pocketknives address their owners, it told me so, but it was by no means a personification. Perhaps in the same way the clock just *told* me that it is 11:30. "Didn't you use my blade," it said, "to carve a heart into the bark of a tree, and then carve A+B into the heart?" It's possible! Quite possible. But it would have been better if even then I had slit my wrists. Or if I had thrown the knife deep into the underbrush. Now I would be safe. From a purely mathematical point of view, nothing in this world changes: people are born, grow up and die; the time in between birth and death they fill by doing and saying the same things done and said by countless numbers of people before them. Everything is just so general. The newspaper, for example. Things are always the same there: on the first page, the speeches of politicians, on the second there is news from the domestic scene and the world; then catastrophes, accidents and murders; stories for the afternoon on the same topics; on the last pages the death notices and the "In Memoriam" column. Only the dates and names change. So why then, if I already know all of that, am I so desperate over being lost in the supermarket? What do I have to lose? I think I know the answer: the story needs to have an atmosphere of desperation, so that I can create a certain tension, because today no one reads stories that don't have desperation, blood, sodomy, and violence.

As time passes, I feel an increasing inclination toward mathematics. It is so consistent. Insensitive. There is not a single lie in mathematics. Love, friendship, compassion—all of them bring on piles and piles of lies. None of that in mathematics. That's because God is a mathematician. However, mathematicians of this world do lie. I am the greatest philosopher who ever walked the face of the earth, and in the end I got lost in the supermarket. But now, I piss on philosophy. Mathematics is what attracts me now. In the end, when God does His reckoning, there will be no emotion, no figures of speech, evidence or counterevidence. None of that. Only pure arithmetic. I already mentioned that God shows no favor toward a single one of the sciences taught at the universities. He even sent word through his son for the wise to be careful. Yet, the wise don't care for warnings. They go on writing their scientific arguments, their dissertations. Fine, we'll see each other at the end of the world when I am resurrected from this pile of beef stew cans, facial cream, old-fashioned candles and O.B. tampons.

God tells me over the phone: pay attention to the past! That won't be an easy thing to do. I have a pile of pasts, but all of them are in such disorder, it all looks like some back-corner office full of unfinished requests and problems, there is too little of the present for me to make order out of what happened, and worst of all, the present keeps flowing into the past. I'll have to do something about it. There is no point in waiting for death. I have other plans for *after death*. However, as soon as I turn to face the past, that whole circus brings tears to my eyes. So much of it should be forgotten, so many things to make peace with, so many things to simply get over. Better if I don't even talk about it. It won't help me at all. That's how it is with stories. You think up an effective beginning and start writing, and then it just goes on and no one knows where it will end. In the beginning there was just one word. Right? And now? An indescribable noise, an unbearable cacophony that no one can understand. Through all of that babble, being the hero of the story is one of the hardest professions. I envy those heroes whose writers know what they want, who plan everything ahead of time. My writer, if I myself am not the writer, is a disorganized, unpredictable person. You can never be sure what is waiting for you in the next sentence. Since I still haven't lost all hope, I might expect, for instance, that with one stroke of the pen he will get me out of the supermarket, marry me off and give me a happy life, but that hope is all in vain. Even if he overcame the nausea he feels towards marriage and an orderly life, if he married me off and made me happy, within a few sentences of happy life and marital bliss he would have my wife cheat on me with my best friend, and I would hang myself out of desperation. Why don't I just forget all that? There is nothing there, beyond *now*, nothing to tie me to pleasant memories. All mistakes. Mistake after mistake. Please, I have my notebook, everything is documented. It says clearly: "In years ending with 1, 3, 5, 7, 9, I had no luck in love. My loves came unexpectedly and left unexpectedly with my best friends. Usually the girls were named Ana, they were nineteen years old, all of them played the piano. Not especially well, but they all played." Some things just seem to repeat themselves, don't they? I should be happy: hardly anyone ever had as many best friends as I did. Sometimes they call me from Canada, Australia, New Zealand. Even from Nepal. They are all living happily ever after. Like in a fairy tale. In the meantime, the supermarket has filled with noise: forty thieves are chasing Ali Baba. "What are they doing in the supermarket? What does the writer want to say? Why is he interrupting the narrative?" the critics and theoreticians are going to ask. I don't know what Ali Baba and the thieves are doing here. But that is like a fairy tale as well. Isn't it? I thought I had forgiven my friends. My knife is whispering to me: "You didn't, you didn't!" That means I didn't. There are no more deceptions. There used to be some. A lot of them. As soon as one of the girls would show up, she would say: "Hello, my name is Ana," and immediately everything would be clear to me: I knew that she was nineteen and that she played the piano. Then again, I don't know why, some little voice would say to me: maybe this time, maybe there won't be any more deceptions. Nonsense! I did everything I could to prevent repetition of the past. What could I do? I should have known that I MYSELF was there so that the past could repeat itself. They would go away with my friends late at night and there was nothing I could do about it. I could have stayed awake. I didn't sleep. But that didn't change anything. The train they took when going away arrived according to schedule at the moment when sleep would overwhelm me. To be quite honest, there was nothing I could do. Let's say that it was not destiny, but just the writer's rather commonplace whim. He wanted them all to be named Ana, to play the piano, to go away with my best friends. Nobody can do a thing about it. That is artistic freedom. The Constitution is on his side. And yet, what if I myself am the writer (which I honestly suspect is true)? In that case, does that mean that the hand of fate is involved in all of this? The writer, most certainly, would have something to say about that, and since I cannot say anything— perhaps because I am obsessed with whether *most certainly* should have been put in apposition—that means I am not the writer. Logically it seems accurate. It would be better just to forget it all completely. There was nothing I could do then. There is much less that I can do now. Why am I struggling with it so? And I was thinking: it would be so easy to just forget it all. In truth, it seemed that all the Anas had left forever: the midnight trains were impudently passing by even before I dropped off to sleep. There was no longer any reason for them to be sneaking around.

It is clearly written: "Usually, after their departure, I would never see them again. If I did see one of them again (never more than one at a time), then it was as two trains passed each other, in some far away place, at a speed of at least 60 mph." But perhaps it only seemed to me that I saw them for an instant through the train car windows. If someone were to ask me where I was going on those trains, I wouldn't know how to answer. Probably those trips were thought up by the author himself just to keep me believing that I had seen one of the Anas. Did I have a proper train ticket? How did I get back to my point of origin? Nothing was said about that. Anyway, that was the Railway Company's problem. Yes, I do remember, occasionally I would talk with the railway inspectors about New Prose. Things weren't so black on those trips. I met some interesting inspectors. From them I learned quite a lot about Joyce and Beckett.

The clock put its hands together to show midnight for a moment. Didn't I once, around midnight, in an attempt to take that last, decisive step, didn't I stop by the phone, ostensibly to take a deep breath, but in fact hoping that it would ring, that I would hear from the receiver one of the many alto voices which I will never be able to forget? It would not be honest to say that the telephone never rang—to that extent one must respect good old realism—it did ring from time to time, but it was always the worried, squeaky voice of my aunt who would ask: are you going to work regularly? Are you washing your hands before you eat? Did you pay your rent? Why don't you call? Is it raining there? Do you have a stomachache? Are you saying your prayers before you go to bed? My answers, for example: I'm going, I'm washing them, I paid it, I don't have time, it's raining, I do, I pray. I never went to see my aunt in person, and she was always so concerned about me. I don't even know where she lives. I actually don't even know if she is still alive. One day, if I make peace with the world, if I get out of the supermarket, I will go and see my aunt. Of course, this should be understood only as a dose of black humor. In no way as a promise. Black humor is one of the rare things which attracts the average reader. Then they repent for falling into the trap like the ultimate fool. If only I had been a few sweet words less sentimental, I would leave all this behind and I would be free. Then this story would not be possible. It would simply not exist.

It happened. The author used a momentary lapse in my attention and married me off. My wife's name is Ana, she's nineteen and, of course, she plays the piano. Poorly, but she plays. I know that I am in the supermarket, that it was not just an ugly dream; I know that the writer just changed the decor and that my wife will leave with my best friend, but — isn't it absurd — again hope arises: maybe this time, maybe this time there won't be any deceptions. In vain is this hope of mine. As I already said, after just a few sentences of happy life, he got bored with the whole thing and set it up so that Ana would leave with my best friend.

Sandoz and Ana are standing next to their packed suitcases.

"Sandoz, I didn't think you were going to be one of them."

Sandoz looks at the ground.

"Love is blind," he says.

The train is slowly creeping into the station.

Of course, I am desperate. I want to hang myself. Like hell! It is not that easy. First I have to wake up, to find a rope. I fell asleep long ago, but I just can't stop talking. My dreams are nonsense, but I keep talking about other nonsense. There is no peace in sleep. There is no peace at all. The story must continue to flow. He has decided to write a thirty-page story. I don't know if I'm dreaming or if it really is true: I have the impression that I am the only one living in the whole world. I'm waiting in vain for Monday. The supermarket will never open its doors again. No one will wake up to turn the page on the calendar. People are just rubber dolls with sad glassy eyes. But the nonsense must continue to flow. Whatever the cost. All of this, this entire collection of stories, it doesn't take more than two hours of reading. What shall I do with my memories which reach back only seventy odd pages into the past. I have to think things up. Everything I say is just make-believe. But the critics, those tubercular moths, will still find something for themselves. I shouldn't be so mean to the critics. I really shouldn't. Only they will take my sadness seriously, my desolation, my loneliness. None of that is worth a red cent, but again it is sad and desolate. I am alone. Is *my* writer alone? I suppose he is. I know that somehow. Not all connections are irreversibly broken. Perhaps I can even imagine him: he's sitting at the desk in the corner of the room; the light from the lamp with the green lampshade only spreads over the sheet of paper and nothing else. I cannot see his face. That's understandable. I can't see anything, I can say *I see* but not that I see. I can't even imagine his face. That's understandable. No, no, that's not understandable. I feel that sometimes he gets up from the desk, he takes a few steps around the room, he drinks a sip of tea and returns to his writing. I would really love it if I could tell him that none of that makes any sense. But even if I could tell him that—it would make no sense, because he is writing, he's the one who makes me say that I would like to tell him that it makes no sense. I think that he also knows that it makes no sense. At least it's easier for him. He writes for an hour, two, three at the most, then he goes out somewhere, but I remain here, in these flat monotonous sentences, in the supermarket. He does nothing to make my stay in his story more bearable. If he at least wanted to play word games, to insert some drawings or something. *But no! There are no more drawings!* I wasn't the one who said that, the previous sentence was not spoken by me. Is it possible that the writer has descended from his Parnassus, that he has lost the final distance between literature and life and is saying to me:

"Tell me, what's bothering you?"

"You see," I tell him *confusedly*, making a *terrible* blunder because it slipped my mind that he is horrified by the adjectives *confused* and *terrible*. "You see, there were so many things I wanted to ask you, and now, when I finally have the opportunity, I have nothing to say. For example, this: who am I? I have a lot of memories, but it seems that they do not belong to me. At certain moments I thought I was you. God addressed me with: O poet! Then I thought I was Bob Horn. I don't know why. Do you know who I am? If you do know, why are you hiding it? Why won't you tell me?"

"I don't know, I really don't know who you are. I only know that you are lost in the supermarket. And also that you wanted to slit your wrists. But that doesn't mean anything. I don't know who I am either. My name also doesn't mean anything. I myself wanted to slit my wrists. That was a few years ago. It was the hand of fate. We are equally lost; you on *that* side, I on *this* side of the paper. You think that I'm omnipotent, that the flow of the story is my whim. I'm telling you it just isn't so. I don't know why the story started as it did, nor do I know how it will end. I only know that it *must* continue. It has to be thirty pages long. Be patient. We're almost halfway there."

And then silence again. The worst thing in stories is that you can never be sure if you were talking to someone else, or just to yourself. Perhaps because in a story there are only two dimensions. Something is missing. Was I talking to the author or was all that just the usual effect of something being made unusual? The clock, safe high up on the wall, spreads its hands and indicates that it is *impossible*.

I exist after all. Once long ago, long ago by the criteria of this clock, I had to be born. All right, birth brings about problems and pain, but all that is quickly forgotten. The worst thing is that you are helpless because your loved ones will not leave you alone, but rather sooner or later they try to make you similar to them. First they give you a name, usually a stupid one, then they force you to *learn* that you are that name, to identify yourself completely with that name. Like clowns they walk by your cradle saying, "I'm your mom, I'm your dad." And it's easy to trick babies. Especially when adults have free rein and unlimited time to dedicate. Blind faith in parental authority is leading this world to destruction. However, how can one expect little children to realize that fathers and mothers are not wise, but that they are rather — like mannequins — repeating the same old story.

I see my mom coming from far away on roller skates, probably from the farmers' market, carrying a basket full of vegetables. How long ago was that? Long before the beginning of this story. Long before the beginning of many stories. The braids in

mom's black hair look like ribbons on a sailor's cap to me. That
was before they built all these supermarkets. I would say that I
was a marvelous child, I washed my hands before meals, recit-
ed the Lord's Prayer, gave up my seat to the elderly and didn't
masturbate, but perhaps I was an evil boy who stole eggs from
the nest, killed white mice and skinned them, but it could also
be that all of that is just the author's intervention because, as we
have already said, books today which don't have evil, blood, per-
version, and violence don't sell very well. Or maybe not, there's
no reason to flee from the guilt any more, I WAS THE ONE who
wrote all this, whoever that *I* might be. Cowardice overcame me.
I forgot that my conflict with the world is irrevocable. I know
that I can't harm *it* but, as long as I keep writing I will keep trying to expose this hypocritical world, whose entire machinery is
focused on creating webs of impossible circumstances, leading
to the meeting of two creatures, a meeting which at the same
moment, unrestrained, hurtles into parting. One should not deceive oneself: I am talking, or he is writing, so that the story will
be sold more easily and thus, I suppose, the memory again appears: I see my mom on roller skates. She is coming from afar,
she stumbles, falls, the vegetables scatter, from her knee blood is
running which will be quite attractive to the average reader. My
grandmother pulls at her hair, my aunt drops her knitting; they
feel uncomfortable—exposed to the looks of readers who are en-
joying someone else's pain. My father cannot stand the shame.
From the drawer of his desk he takes out his government-issued
military pistol and fires a shot into his temple. The readers are
wondering: was that enough of a reason for suicide? I bear up
under it all philosophically. It should not be forgotten that I am
the greatest philosopher who ever walked the face of the earth,
making fun of *it*, which is why that world itself is taking its revenge by making me get lost in the supermarket. In spite of it
all, I felt sorry for my father. That romantic fool believed blindly in a better tomorrow. He was an optimist. There are others
like him. A better tomorrow. It exists—it would be nihilistic to
claim otherwise—but the organization of the world is such that

a man must always die *today*. My father killed himself in a certain *today*, and it was already a better tomorrow. My grandma said: "Drunken fool"; my aunt said: "Oh, it's so romantic." My mom looked good in black. My father's death revived her. She finished her medical studies, did a specialization in psychiatry and became a real lady. She never used roller skates again.

I doubt, I doubt that I will manage to hold up for all thirty pages. It's too much for me. If I can just make it to page XX, then later I'll worry about how to go on after that. Time is passing; the clock tells me it's already 2:30. I no longer feel even the slightest intolerance toward it. I must admit: the time of my disappearance will be my own fabrication. The clocks are only here as props. When I think about it more carefully, it wasn't *time* that irritated me about the clock. No! I was angry because it was so boring, because it kept repeating the same thing endlessly: tick-tock, tick-tock. It's pronounced that *tick-tock* at least a million times since I've been here. I kept quiet for the rest of the night but it just kept babbling, until it finally showed me that it was 5:55 and that the supermarket would open soon. Finally! *SOMETHING* was crooked. No wonder. I sat on it all night long. I straightened it up so that it was SOMETHING again. I'll never know what it was. I put everything back in its place. I didn't steal anything. Nobody can blame me for anything. I stretched, and headed for the exit. The cashier looked at me dubiously. "Two SUPER SILVER razor blades," I said. "Anything else?" she asked. "No, nothing else. That will be all."

Before I went out, I looked up at the clock. It seized the chance, and with its second hand it quickly showed me that to the end of the story only *one second* remained . . .

An Unauthorized and Completely Unsolicited Biography of Svetislav Basara

If the cartographers are correct, which is the subject of a debate that will not be taken up here, there is supposedly a small town in southwestern Serbia called Bajina Bašta, just across the Drina River from Bosnia. There, in the wee hours of a morning in the year 5714 (1953 according to the Gregorian calendar), Svetislav Basara was born for the first time in this life. Or maybe he was not. Perhaps he just materialized in the first grade with his pencils and paper, ready to set off on his long and tortuous road to salvation, to his destiny as a prevaricator for the reading public. Only history can tell, and history is not saying much these days.

He spent a happy childhood in Bajina Bašta and in another, only slightly less dubious, town named Užice. He played the guitar, drank, and chased girls. He finished his so-called secondary education, or his education finished him, at the age of eighteen. Or perhaps nineteen, but that is unimportant. He played in a rock band and wrote songs. That is important. But the band broke up. Their equipment was poor and they had no money to buy anything better. So, he moved to the infamous outskirts of Belgrade where he lived in a pickled-cabbage barrel with some people he did not know. Who he would never get to know. Because, as he discovered quickly, no one ever really knows anyone else. Except in the biblical sense. He did know some people in that sense. Or perhaps he did not. At least not until later. He went to college for a while, but the environment disturbed him, so he sought renovation and rebirth along other avenues. The dirty boulevard. Those were the decrees of Fortuna's Wheel. Unemployed, down on his luck, he went to the library, as any other vagrant would do. He started to write.

He published some poetry and a little book of short stories called *Vanishing Tales*. Then he drank some beer and moved out of the barrel into a closet in some other, equally ignominious suburb of Belgrade. He drank some cognac and moved back home. He smoked a cigarette. He continued to write.

With the publication of *Through the Looking-Glass Cracked*, he found his literary niche. The book caused the first tectonic shifts in the otherwise shaky foundations of Serbian "historical" prose. The reading public was fascinated and disturbed. Who was this young writer who dared to tilt at the sacred windmills of Serbian pseudo-history, pseudo-culture, and pseudo-myth? More importantly, *Through the Looking-Glass Cracked* laid the foundation for another book, *The Cyclist Conspiracy*, which challenged not only "institutionalized" prose, but also the "postmodernist" school, with Milorad Pavić at the forefront. Basara had come into his own.

In the literary circles of a monumentally worrisome country named Yugoslavia, and especially in the practically non-existent country named Serbia, he is known as the "enfant terrible." The reasons for this are disputable, but it may have something to do with the fact that he is a talented narrator. It goes without saying that, once that first label was stapled to his forehead, a plethora of others would soon follow. Things have gone too far! Basara now looks like a telephone pole at election time: posters, labels, telephone numbers, pictures of political candidates, lost-and-found notices, all flapping from him in the wind. Nihilist, anarchist, postmodernist, bad patriot, naughty boy, sexist, chauvinist, prophet, demagogue, philanthropist, good patriot, revisionist, bohemian, librarian, writer ... the list of labels goes on and on. However, only one label has ever really stuck: person. Svetislav Basara is a person. An authentic one. That is a fact, perhaps the only true fact in this biography so far.

As a writer, he has produced a long list of books in a variety of genres: novels, novellas, short stories, essays and plays. This is also a fact: you can buy them in the bookstores, if they are not sold out. He is something of a cult figure for the younger generations. That's it! That is why he is the *enfant terrible*! Svetislav Basara writes in a style that goes beyond all institutionally and politically correct styles. He does not pay homage to the unities of literature. He believes that space, time and action are only illusions. No! His characters—they are the ones who do not believe in space, time and action. Basara would not go so far. Or he would go even farther. There are other, much more important things to believe in. Basara's writings deal with the relationship between truth and illusion, between humankind and history, and between people and their perspectives. He asks the question which is perhaps most important of all: are we really present here and now, or can we live in alternative heres and nows which are far more important for the development of civilization and culture? Basara contends that modern man has set off along the wrong road in its denial of spiritual matters and their true place in life. And life is just too short, or perhaps too long, to do that.

In ever-more-distant Belgrade, Basara moved into a shoebox. He jousted with the system, with all systems, armored in his love for the truth and for humankind. He just cannot and will not shut up. So, they sent him to Cyprus as an ambassador. Maybe that would shut him up once and for all?! No! He returned to Belgrade after drinking a lot of wine and writing a book about Nietzsche and Cyprus, and later, to everyone's chagrin, he won the highest literary prize in Serbia for his book *The Rise and Fall of Parkinson's Disease*. Now he could finally be silent. Or not.

Alas, even as I write these lines, even as you read them, he is smoking a cigarette. And he continues to write.

Randall Major, 2015

Svetislav Basara's Published Works

Vanishing Tales, 1982 (short stories)
The Chinese Letters, 1985 (novel)
Peking by Night, 1985 (short stories)
Through the Looking-Glass Cracked, 1986 (novella)
On the Edge, 1987 (essays)
The Cyclist Conspiracy, 1988 (novel)
Phenomena, 1989 (short stories)
In Search of the Grail, 1990 (novel)
The Mongolian Travel Guide, 1992 (novel)
Dark Side of the Moon, 1992 (essays)
Vanishing Tales and Political Writings, 1993 (short stories)
De Bello Civili, 1993 (novella)
Selected Stories, 1994 (short stories)
Vexland, 1995 (novel)
The Tree of Life, 1995 (essays)
The Virtual Cabala, 1996 (essays)
Looney Tunes, 1997 (novel)
Collected Plays, 1997 (plays)
Civil War Within, 1998 (translation of *De Bello Civili*, 1993)
Holy Lard, 1998 (novel)
The Wolf's Lair, 1998 (essays)
The Ideology of Heliocentrism, 1999 (essays)
The Illusion Machines, 2000 (interviews and essays)
John B. Malkovitch, 2001 (novel)
The Best Stories of Svetislav Basara, 2001 (anthology)
Chinese Letter, 2004 (translation of *Kinesko Pismo*, 1985)
The Heart of the Earth, 2004 (novel)
Phantom Pain, 2005 (novel)
The Rise and Fall of Parkinson's Disease, 2006 (novel, received the NIN Award)
Lost in the Supermarket, 2008 (anthology of short stories)
Monkeying Around, 2008 (short stories)
The Diary of Marta Koen, 2008 (novel)
The Cyclist Conspiracy, 2009/2012 (novel, translation of *Fama o biciklistima*, 1988)
The Secret History of Bajina Bašta, 2010 (novel)
Mein Kampf, 2011 (novel)
Longevity, 2012 (novel)
Filth, 2013 (novel)
A Little This, a Little That, 2014 (correspondence)
Angel of Assassination, 2015 (novel)

(translations of titles provisional)